Puddlebrain

Shaun Allan

ISBN-13: 978-1-910484-13-5
ISBN-10: 1-91-048413-X

in association with

Myrddin Publishing Group

www.myrddinpublishinggroup.com

*****

Dedication

To Ripley for your magic and madness.

*****

Acknowledgments

Puddlebrain took a little time to write. Meaning, a lot. I started the book whilst writing Sin and didn't really know where it was going to go. I just had the 'baby' witch and no powers. Puddlebrain's name came to me immediately, with her sisters' following quickly after, except Gemini was almost called Gemima.

Because Sin doesn't really know how to shut up, he chased off the witches, letting them have the time to find their magic themselves. That didn't happen, but the dust left in his wake covered their tracks. It was much more recently that I found the beginnings of the story again, re-read it and realised I still really liked it.

Puddlebrain is much like Sin. OK, she's a witch and 352 years old, but they're both forced into circumstances they can't control. Sin has Joy. Puddlebrain has Billy. Sin has his powers and doesn't want them, Puddlebrain doesn't have hers and wishes she did.

With Puddlebrain, the rain dances with her. With Sin, it drowns him in a tsunami.

See? Almost twinsies.

Well, on her road through the Grimace and back again, Pudders, as she's never called, was helped by persons other than just a grumpy gnome. So thank you to all who gave the push I needed. I hope Puddlebrain spins her magic into your hearts.

Contents

Acknowledgments iv

Prologue 1

Chapter One 2

Chapter Two 7

Chapter Three 13

Chapter Four 19

Chapter Five 24

Chapter Six 27

Chapter Seven 31

Chapter Eight 34

Chapter Nine 41

Chapter Ten 45

Chapter Eleven 50

Chapter Twelve 56

Chapter Thirteen 60

Chapter Fourteen 64

Chapter Fifteen 66

Chapter Sixteen 71

Chapter Seventeen 76

Chapter Eighteen 82

Chapter Nineteen 84

Chapter Twenty 90

Chapter Twenty One 93

Chapter Twenty Two 97

Chapter Twenty Three 101

Chapter Twenty Four 104

Chapter Twenty Five 109

Chapter Twenty Six 114

Chapter Twenty Seven 120
Chapter Twenty Eight 124
Chapter Twenty Nine 130
Chapter Thirty 136
Chapter Thirty One 140
Chapter Thirty Two 145
Chapter Thirty Three 150
Chapter Thirty Four 155
Chapter Thirty Five 158
Chapter Thirty Six 164
Chapter Thirty Seven 167
Chapter Thirty Eight 174
Chapter Thirty Nine 179
Chapter Forty 186
Chapter Forty One 191
Chapter Forty Two 193
Epilogue 195
About the Author 197

Prologue

A shadow isn't your friend. It's not a piece of you that's always there, like your arm or your head. It isn't your partner when you're lonely or something to run with on a sunny day.

A shadow steals the light.

A shadow steals the night.

And a shadow can steal more.

Much more.

Chapter One

Hubble, bubble, toil and trouble. Lig of legwort and bald man's stubble. So the witches' cauldron bubbled.

"Is that soup ready yet?"

"Quit yer whining! It'll be ready when it's ready. Until then it won't."

"But I'm hungry!"

"I'm not surprised! It's been a whole ten minutes since you last stuffed your face!"

Edna, Gemini and Puddlebrain. Three sisters. Three witches. Three right royal pains in the posterior. They bickered and twittered and argued almost constantly, but such was their way. Let any man dare to even so much as raise his voice and they'd show him! In the flick of a finger he'd be turned into a frog, make no mistake. Then he'd learn.

Well, no they wouldn't. Actually they wouldn't turn him into anything at all. The witches would not so much as make his hair purple or plonk a great big hairy wart on the end of his nose, looking like it was ready to jump off and grow another person

But they'd not be very happy, rest assured!

The witches were sitting around their kitchen table, a rickety old heap of rough-hewn logs that looked as if it was held together simply because it couldn't decide whether or not to fall apart. It was thirteen o'clock and it was lunch time. Gemini was hungry, but this wasn't unusual. As Edna had pointed out, or had at least thought of pointing out, it could have been three minutes past seven on a Sunday morning and Gemini would be hungry. It could be twenty-four minutes to fifteen or seventy-five minutes past thirty-four and she would *still* be hungry. Gemini was forever hungry. She didn't always eat, but she always felt like she wanted to. This led to her being in permanent grumblemode which, on occasion, got on her sisters nerves. It didn't matter, though, because everything the sisters did got on the other ones' nerves.

They liked it that way.

None of the sisters could tell the time. They couldn't grasp the idea of there only being twenty four hours in a day. It just didn't give you enough time to do *anything*. Why not have sixty or ninety five hours? Whose duffered idea was it to have a daft number like twenty four? They couldn't understand it, so simply didn't take any notice. Thirteen o'clock was always about half way through the day, and it was always lunch time, much to Gemini's delight. They had lived around four hundred years apiece (well, three hundred and fifty two in the case of Puddlebrain, the baby, bless her) and had never given Time more than a passing nod of recognition. As long as they kept out of each other's way, that was fine by them. Mostly that's what happened.

Well, there was that one time…

"Is the soup ready yet?" whined Gemini.

"It wasn't ready two minutes ago and I doubt very much if it's going to be ready in two minutes time," Edna sighed. She was the cook of the family and was fair rushed off her feet trying to cope with her sister's perpetual appetite. "Why don't you chew your toenails for a while until I serve it up? You haven't had a good chew for ages and they look like they could do with one."

Gemini looked down at her bare feet. Her sister had a point. Her toenails could do with a good munch. The thing was, it meant she had to bend over to reach them, and she wasn't as trim as she used to be. It took effort and her stomach was already protesting at having to wait so long for food. Maybe Puddlebrain would do the honours. Gemini asked her.

Puddlebrain had been dozing. She was becoming increasingly tired of the constant arguments that bounced around the house like a crazed ping pong ball, full of energy and tightly contained destruction. She hadn't had a good night's sleep for over a century and just wanted to flake out somewhere dark and quiet. Just an hour or seven, that'd be nice. She thought about her sister's request. If it would keep the peace for even a few minutes, it was probably worth it. Trouble was, toenails always got caught in your teeth. Puddlebrain hated that.

"Oh, just magic them short!" she replied.

Edna and Gemini looked at her as if they'd been slapped across the face.

"Just *magic* them short!" Edna repeated, snorting through her nose (an unpleasant habit she'd developed after an accident with a broom thirty years earlier).

"Ner *nerner* ner ner!" Gemini repeated the repeat.

"Very funny," said Edna, obviously not thinking it was funny at all.

"Indeed," said Gemini, obviously thinking the same.

Puddlebrain sighed. It was Halloween soon. Maybe this year would be different.

"Maybe this year will be different," she said out loud, not needing to be more specific. Her sisters would know exactly what she was talking about.

"Yes. Maybe this year will be different. Maybe it will." Edna snorted again, making it clear she was actually thinking *'And pigs can swim backwards! Of course it won't be different. It'll be exactly the same as every year. Halloween will come and go and our powers will stay gone.'*

"Ner *nerner* ner ner!" Gemini said again. She wasn't the fastest mop in the bucket and couldn't always be relied on to think of something witty and intelligent to say. Generally she stayed with the reliable last clever remark she'd chanced upon.

The sky outside had spent the morning trying to decide whether or not to rain and looking like it couldn't really be bothered to do either. Now it seemed to have made up its mind and started to hammer at the window in great blobs that splatted like spit on a broomstick.

"Oh, shut up!" Edna shouted at the air.

The rain suddenly eased to a more sedate drizzle. The sky was dark. It was definitely sulking, but Edna ignored it. She just couldn't be doing with huffy weather. Halloween was only a few days away and they still had to boil their soup over an open fire. Long gone were the days of flicking a finger and having a nice three course meal plonked down in front of you before you could say "I'm a dingdong." Nowadays a simple snack took… well, normal time! It just wasn't on. Edna decided to join the sky in a spot of sulking.

It wasn't fair. Thanks, Puddlebrain, for being a right puddlebrain and reminding them all of that.

Puddlebrain took the frown and stuck-out lower lip of her sister as a cue to be elsewhere. She stood up.

"I'm going to bed," she said.

"It's only 13 o'clock! What about your food?" Gemini asked.

"You have it." Puddlebrain told her as she walked through to her room.

"I suppose I'll chew my own toenails then?" Gemini called.

There was no answer, but Gemini had forgotten about it already. Edna was pouring large ladles of chicken and bladderwrack soup into a dish. Gemini wasn't that keen on chicken – it kept her awake at night thinking she should crow when dawn came. The problem was Dawn, the sugar-and-spice-and-all-things-nasty-and-slimy lady, only called on a Thursday afternoon, which meant Gemini had a sleepless night for nothing. No matter. The bladderwrack, with its festering podules boiled to just the right temperature, was more than enough to take the edge off the broth.

Chapter Two

Edna used to be very good at potions. Once upon a long time ago, the eldest of the sisters was the queen of concoctions and the matron of making bubbly things in cauldrons. There was no ailment she couldn't cure (or cause) and her reputation had spread far and wide. She made a nice tidy profit from the small store she opened up in the front room of their house. A dozen customers a day would tread through the always-open front door, hoping and expecting that Edna could solve their problems for them.

Generally she did just that. She was normally kind and helpful. Occasionally though, with no warning whatsoever, Edna would decide to be decidedly *un*kind and *un*helpful. It was usually only a brief lapse, but that was all it took to 'accidentally' substitute, for example, rat's *tail* for rat's *ear.* Well, imagine! A humble paying customer would want to clear up a nasty rash and instead end up sprouting an extra toe. It didn't go down too well. OK, so an accident was accidental (as accidents usually are), but when the mayor found he could only walk backwards between three o'clock and half past seven, it simply had to stop.

Banning a witch from using her magic was like telling the sun not to rise in the morning. It was like telling sheep not to dip or corn not to flake. Apart from the fact that she'd say "Stuff you!" just before turning you into a frog, a witch couldn't *not* use her magic. It was part of them. It was more natural than breathing. It was instinct.

Besides, they liked doing magicky things. Why should they stop? And try making one do that!

The mayor, an ever-smartly dressed man who seemed to roll when he walked, thought to take it upon himself to stop the 'wicked' witches from performing their black arts. He conveniently forgot that Edna had previously given him a lush, full head of hair, had cured his wife of some extremely unsightly boils (which, granted, Edna had caused in the first place), and had turned his daughter into a beautiful young woman from the, well, homely girl that she was.

Mayor Harper approached the front gate to the witches' garden all beefed up with his own self-importance. His chest was out, although it was hard to tell over his Honourable Rotundness, and his nose was high. A gaggle of his cronies waddled on behind. Behind them prowled what would have been a mob of angry villagers if more than a slack handful had been courageous enough to face the wrath of the demon witches. Those that did shamble along being Mr. Pompous, sorry, Mayor Harper's entourage were only really there for the show they were sure would ensue.

Mayor Harper, Kenny to those who liked him and Harpy to those who didn't (which, pretty much, meant no one called him Kenny, especially since his name was Jeremy), paused at the gate. Bravado was one thing, stupidity was entirely another. He'd persuaded the villagers, or at least some of them, that the witches had to be stopped. Yes, his argument was with Edna, but all three were witches and, as such, all three were responsible for the countless number of times he walked into a wall or tripped over a stone because, between three and seven thirty, he could only walk in reverse.

At a town meeting the previous night, only a dozen or so had turned up to hear his plea and not all of those had appeared today. He wasn't disappointed though. Harpy didn't quite see things the way everyone else did. As far as he was concerned, the lack of any decent turnout simply implied that his villagers thought he was man enough to handle the situation on his own. Some, though he didn't know it, actually thought he was big enough for two men, or maybe even three on a good day and after a hearty breakfast.

He held onto the gate, steeling himself for the task ahead. As far as he knew, Edna and her sisters were normally friendly. They lived quietly alone in their tidy, if small, home. They wouldn't say boo to a goose, although he had witnessed the youngest one, Puddlebrain, having a lengthy conversation with one once. He didn't really expect any trouble, but he was quite prepared to face any that might come trotting along. He was mayor. He could handle it.

His pudgy hand pushed open the gate. He expected it to creak as it moved, but it didn't. It wasn't going to give him the satisfaction. Harpy stepped through into the front garden and began to walk to the house. He glanced back briefly to check that his followers were doing just that - following. They weren't. He felt so proud! They had the utmost confidence in him too! He smiled to himself.

Right, witches, here I come.

The path he was on was smooth, polished stone. It kept itself clean and was proud, almost to the point of being vain, of its appearance. The path knew who might be an unwelcome visitor and knew just how to handle such guests. Sometimes, particularly on lazy summer's days, it might meander for a while, pausing here and there around the garden to give whoever might be walking it time to have a leisurely stroll. Other times, such as during a harsh winter's blizzard, it would lead slap-bang straight to the door, hurrying you along so you didn't get too wet or frozen to the bone.

In the case of Mayor Harper, the path led a merry figure eight and ended up right where it started. Before he knew it, he was going back the way he came, facing, once again, his brood. He turned around and frowned. The path was, once more, straight to the door. Not one to give up easily, he started again towards the house. Persistent was how he thought of it. Stubborn as a mule with a bad hair day who soooo didn't wanna pull that plough and wasn't going to no matter how many carrots you bribed him with was how almost everybody else thought of him.

By the third time, he was beginning to lose his patience. He didn't exactly have too much of that to begin with. Patience is supposedly a virtue and Mayer Harpy was far from a virtuous man. He only became Mayor because no-one else could be bothered to spare their Sunday afternoons to go knocking on doors canvassing for votes. It had been an almost unanimous victory at the election – unanimous in that out of those who actually made the effort to put their cross on the slip, only three had voted for the other candidate, Burner, the donkey who pulled the plough over in Farmer Hopkins' south field. Of course, Harpy insisted, his majority vote had nothing to do with the fact that his name was at the top of the slip and no-one had read any further down. They had *faith!* He would prove them right, he decided. He would show them he could live up to their expectations. Well. The villagers' expectations of Jeremy Harper had certainly been lived up to. Harpy, Mule and Pompous were only a few of the… compliments aimed at his Heftiness.

Mayor Harper was becoming rather rosy faced. If he'd have been a kettle, steam would have been hissing from his ears and his eyes would have been boiling. This was a thought that occurred to Edna as she hid with her sisters behind the curtains of their front room. They weren't hiding out of fear, oh no. They were simply enjoying the waddlesome one's predicament. They were justifiably proud of their path and would see to it that it was rewarded with a nice scrub and polish before the day was out.

"Come on Edna," Gemini said. "Get rid of him. Send him packing on his way. It's almost thirteen o'clock."

Gemini was hungry for a change. She didn't want anything to interrupt feeding time at the zoo. Puddlebrain, who had joined them to see what the fuss was about, for once agreed with her sister.

"Just give him what he wants and he'll be happy," she said. Granted, she was laughing along with her sisters, but she knew the mayor wouldn't be happy. They were witches and, while they were normally treated with friendship, she knew there was always a hint of mistrust from the villagers. The mayor was an ass, rather than a mule, but he could make things particularly awkward for them if he had half a mind, which was about all he did have.

"Oh, I suppose so," Edna sighed. "Spoil my fun, why don't you? And it's already been thirteen o'clock, Gemini. Twice. You're just being greedy."

Gemini looked sheepish. She was a growing girl. She couldn't help having a healthy appetite.

Edna stood back from the window and brushed herself down. She would greet the mayor with all the sweetness and light she could muster, mister. She would apologise profusely for her 'accident' and would put it right with a flick of her finger. And he wouldn't grow the donkey's tail for a good three months.

"How do I look?"

"Divine," said Gemini. She meant it too. Edna was only three minutes older, but was so much more confident and self-assured. Gemini couldn't help but look up to her. Edna knew she was, basically, her sister's hero and took every opportunity to milk the situation like a farmer tending his prize cow.

"Like you mean business," Puddlebrain said. Being the youngest, and made to remember that fact by various comments, she still had a rebellious streak in her. It kept her from fawning too much at either of her sisters, although she liked and respected them immensely. The arguments that flew around the house between them like bats in a belfry were signs of how much they loved rather than hated one another. In this instance, Edna knew her stuff. They were all skilled witches, but Edna was in a league of her own.

"Right," Edna said. "Let's go get him."

"Don't do anything… unreasonable now," Puddlebrain said.

"Me? As if."

Gemini and Puddlebrain looked at each other. As if, indeed.

Edna walked purposefully towards the front door, which, naturally, opened for her. The door had forgotten to do its job once before and Gemini had ended up with a sizable lump on her forehead. The door never made that mistake again, not once its splinters had healed anyway.

Chapter Three

Gather round, ladeees 'n' genalmen. Roll up!

In the red corner, we have Mr. Pomp... Mayor Harper, mayor and snob extraordinaire, weighing in at two pigs and a donkey. In the blue corner, we have Edna, witch and occasional teapot collector, weighing in at two pigs, three mice and a chicken.

Mayor Harper stopped dead in his tracks. Well, he wasn't dead, and he hadn't made any tracks – any dirt that had been inconsiderate enough to fall on the path immediately jumped off (it could get rather angry when pushed), but his pause was fairly pronounced. He was not, as has been noted, stupid. The sight of Edna striding from the depths of her house with thunder thundering across her face was enough to stop the rain in its fall or the sun in its shine. Mayor Roly stopped in his poley. When he saw the other two wicked witches crawl out behind their sister, he very nearly turned on his tail and did his best to run. His better judgement didn't get the better of him in this case, so he stood his ground and waited.

"Mayor."

"Edna."

"Hello."

"Hello indeed."

"Well, that's the unpleasantries over with. To what do I owe this distinct pleasure?"

Edna emphasised her sarcasm with a little wave of her finger. It had the desired effect and Harpy took a step back. He then remembered he was an idiot and stepped forward again. He was not going to be scared off by a silly woman who just happened to be able to give him a second head. That wouldn't have been so bad, but the first head wasn't much good to begin with.

Edna smiled. He was good, she'd give him that. Harpy might not have been the quickest shake of the lamb's tail, but he was plainly courageous. Either that or he really was the dunderhead that everyone believed. Puddlebrain stepped to her right hand side and Gemini flanked her left. They were smiling too. Edna knew they would leave this up to her, but their added menace was making this much more fun. Harpy's face slowly changed from the rosy red it had been to a distinctly sickly white. The thick thatch of jet-black hair on his voluminous head, a present from Edna only weeks before, served to make his pallid skin look like an anaemic snowman's. All he needed was a carrot nose and a couple of lumps of coal for eyes.

Hmmm, thought Edna. *That was a thought…*

"I've come to instruct you to cease your meddling magic." The mayor took another step forward. He refused to be intimidated by the likes of these. He would show them!

"Have you now. How interesting. Hear that, sisters? He's going to *instruct* us to stop using our magic."

Gemini and Puddlebrain laughed quietly. They were nowhere near as forceful as their sister, and realised it was her fault that things had come to this, but it *was* rather funny. The mayor was going to stop them. The *mayor!* Puddlebrain, years before, had needed to show him how to tie his own shoelaces and he had been so useless at it he had to start wearing buckled shoes. That was when he was a young man, let alone a child.

"How precisely, do you expect to do that then?"

Edna stepped towards the mayor. She didn't need to be close to him to use her magic, and could easily have done without the smell of sweat and baked beans that emanated from his Pudginess, but effect was all important here. He and his loyal band of quivering wrecks needed to be shown - not who was boss, but who was in charge. It wasn't the same thing. The witches could have been across the road, down the street and around the corner and still have turned the mayor into a frog if they'd wished. Harpy was about to be shown that you never cross the road to cross a witch.

They wondered occasionally why the villagers were always so afraid of being turned into frogs. As far as the sisters were concerned, no witch had ever cast such a spell. Witches liked frogs. They certainly wouldn't taint the frog population by adding a few people. What a horrendous thought! Still, it was a rumour that added a little spice to the tales of witches and their ways.

"Oh, do not underestimate me," Harpy said. He turned and smiled at his followers, a little dismayed that they seemed to have backed away from the fence. Oh well, he thought. They would soon see what he was made of. He turned back to face the witches.

Edna was right in front of him, her nose a nostril hair's breadth away from his.

"Boo!"

Harpy did a very unmayorlike thing then. He squealed. Farmer Hopkins' piglets, all eight of them, couldn't make a sound like that even if they were in a singing contest where the Grand Prize was to have as much sloppy mud as you could wallow in. He also quivered. He shook like a rag in a storm. Luckily, well sort of, stupidity took control and he calmed down. He was the MAYOR! She was just a... a witch!

"Boo yourself, witch."

Edna raised an eyebrow thoughtfully. So he *was* denser than Three-Mile Forest. Amazing. She had thought that was just a rumour. She smiled. This would be even more fun. The witch turned and walked slowly back to her siblings.

"What is there to underestimate, Mayor?" she said. "You were only elected because the villagers are a bunch of lazy fools who couldn't care less if a donkey led them, something which would doubtless be an improvement on you."

There were grumbles from the gathering outside the garden. They didn't seem to appreciate being called lazy fools. Gemini and Puddlebrain gasped at their sister's audacity. They assumed she would simply cast a spell and be back in time for afternoon tea. Mayor Harper stepped forward and opened his mouth. He shut it again when he realised he couldn't think of anything to say.

"You dare to come here and threaten me?" Edna continued. She was enjoying herself and it was a fairly safe bet she would have continued even if she had been struck by lightning. "Do you know who I am? *Do you know who I am?* I mended your father's broken leg. I helped nurse your grandmother. I stopped your idiot of a great-grandfather from marrying his pet goat! Obviously you have inherited his great intellect. So tell me, *Mayor*. What is there to underestimate?"

Edna's sisters were stunned. They had never seen Edna quite like this. It was hilarious and frightening at the same time and they didn't quite know what to do. Harpy, meanwhile, had progressively turned deeper and deeper shades of crimson. He opened his mouth three times as if he was going to say something, then shut it each time. His mouth wanted to speak, but his brain couldn't quite come up with anything meaningful. All he managed was a kind of dribbling, gargling sound. There was only one thing he could do, and Edna saw exactly what it was going to be. He couldn't win on a war of words, and he would certainly lose a battle of spells, so a physical attack was all that remained.

Three streets and a fountain away, the village clock chimed.

Mayor Harper breathed in, making him look like an inflated balloon ready to pop.

The clock chimed once more.

Edna raised her finger. She was going to forgo tradition and actually give Harpy green skin, bug eyes, a long tongue and a voice that could only say 'Ribbit,' a word much more intelligent than most that issued from his lips. She would turn him into a frog.

The village clock, an ornate and beautiful piece set in a graceful, if ageing, tower of intricately carved willow, struck a third time.

It was three o'clock, to those that didn't make it up as they went along.

Harpy, despite his impressive bulk, made to surge forward at Edna. Unfortunately, between the grand ol' hours of three and seven thirty, he couldn't actually go forward, surging or otherwise. He fell backwards, tripping over his own feet and landing in an untidy heap at the foot of the gate.

Edna had already flicked her finger before she realised what had happened. The spell streamed from her hand to where the mayor had been a second before. A family of silverfish had been having a quiet birthday get-together in the short grass by the edge of the path. The spell hit them squarely, reflected off them in a wide spread, and flew straight back to its source. It hit the three sisters full on.

Mayor Harpy didn't wait to see what effect it might have. He, finally, realised he wasn't as invincible as he had thought and scrambled to his feet. He and his followers, those that hadn't had the sense to quietly return to their homes already, made haste their retreat. Nothing remained of them but a few chicken bones from Henry Pesterdear, a man who even took snacks in the bath with him. He and Gemini would get on very well in years to come.

The silverfish interrupted their party to briefly comment on the fact that they were no longer silver, but what a lovely shade of green they had turned, before returning to the festivities at hand.

Edna, Gemini and Puddlebrain stood in stunned silence, watching the quickly retreating figures quickly retreat. Gemini's tongue snapped out and caught a passing fly, which she gulped down hungrily.

"Ribbit," said Edna.

Indeed, thought Puddlebrain. "Ribbit!" she said.

The trio turned and hopped back indoors. The door closed behind them.

It was two weeks, three days and seventeen hours (or thereabouts in witch-time) before Gemini could eat bladderwrack stew with custard dumplings again. It was another four days before they could walk without hopping and hitting their heads on the low ceilings and a good five days beyond that before any of them could say anything other than "Ribbit."

Chapter Four

Seventy-five years later, while Gemini was repeatedly moaning about whether the soup was ready, their powers had still not returned. From the day Edna had faced Mayor Harper and turned a partying family of silverfish green, the only thing the witches could turn was the air blue with their curses and arguments. The cauldron, big, black and a shining example to cauldron-hood everywhere, had been Edna's pride and joy but was now nothing more than a soup pan. Their brooms, streamlined for better aerodynamics during flight, were relegated to hunting out stray bits of dust that had forgotten to clean themselves up.

Their fingers, those finely honed tools of hexing flexing, were about as much use as, well, a *normal* person's. They were only good for picking the nose, scratching the head or waggling at each other in the heated midst of yet another argument. Occasionally one of the sisters might manage a weak fizzle at their fingertips, a hint that somewhere inside still hid their magic. This would undoubtedly result in a frenzy of finger flicking, as if they had suddenly formed a band and were madly playing some weird kind of invisible piano. The sisters were, however, about as musical as a brick, and as magical as one too.

In other words they weren't.

Edna, Gemini and Puddlebrain were witches in name only. Their magic seemed to have fled faster than Mayor Plumpalump and they could *not* get it back. Did they try? You bet your sweet potato they did.

Edna did her very best to mix together various potions in an effort to regain their powers, but managed to concoct only a chicken curry at best and rancid batwing broth at worst. Gemini, who at one time could charm the cheese from a cow, had no better luck, but at least her efforts didn't leave a nasty taste in the back of the mouth.

Puddlebrain was different. Puddlebrain was always different.

Edna was, basically, the boss. By virtue of being the oldest, she almost always made the decisions. Gemini was the inbetweeny. She had struggled to find her place in the grand scheme of witchiness and had settled for not being able to tell Edna what to do, but at least being more than able to pick on Puddlebrain. Not being the brightest bulb in the flowerbed had its disadvantages, but she coped, although it was sometimes difficult to see just how she managed to manage. The time she wanted to make it thirteen o'clock all day because she was particularly hungry, but instead made it half past midnight for a week still made her wince.

Puddlebrain was the baby. Even at three hundred and fifty two, which seems so much older than if you write it like 352, she was still mothered by her sisters (in between being picked on by Gemini). She seemed to have been made up of all the bits that had somehow dropped off her sisters. She had the calmness and thoughtfulness that Edna had mislaid and possessed the intelligence and tenderness that Gemini had somehow forgotten even existed. This, in the eyes of her sisters, made her a great big soft Ya-Ya.

None of them actually knew what a Ya-Ya was, but Edna and Gemini both agreed that Puddlebrain was a prime example, and had Ya-Ya-ness in spades. Puddlebrain didn't mind. If this was being a Ya-Ya, then Ya-Ya she was. As far as hexing and charming went, she was a quiet, considerate witch. She preferred to boil a kettle over a flame than wiggle her finger at it. She occasionally, without her sisters knowing it, swept up herself rather than just leave it to the broom. The doors had handles and she actually used them instead of simply expecting the door to open for her.

She could walk out in the pouring rain and not get wet, but that was because the rain liked her and parted as she passed through. If she fancied being soaked, as she did sometimes (splashing in puddles while getting drenched from a downpour was a particular favourite) then the rain would gladly fall on her, occasionally even going out of its way to soak her. Puddlebrain kept most of her powers to herself. She didn't show off like the others often did and even they didn't know exactly what she was capable of, so they chose to think she wasn't very good at anything. A Ya-Ya.

But she was the baby, so it was expected. She'd learn. She'd grow into her finger. Maybe she was just a late developer.

Well, thanks to Edna's little escapade with Mayor Harper, she'd never get the chance.

In the seventy-five years since then, they had tried everything they could think of and nothing had succeeded. If it wasn't for the fact that they had lived for so long and the spice jars in the kitchen kept themselves topped up and in a neat order, you'd think the witches were simply normal people.

Eventually, that's how the villagers came to think of the three strange women who lived at the far end of Shadowmoss Lane. Not quite normal, but getting there. Sort of 'normal' with a side salad of a little bit weird. Mayor Harper had claimed a victory after his encounter, but it didn't fool anyone. He ended up retiring from office only a few weeks later, saying that he had reached the pinnacle of his career in his triumph over the witches, and it was time to pass the mantle of Mayorship on to someone else. A collective sigh of relief was breathed from the village folk and Burner, the donkey, stepped into Harpy's generous boots.

Edna made the move from potions to pancakes (and all manner of other fine delicacies), and Gemini… Gemini stayed pretty much the same. She was basically harmless anyway. Once the witches had accepted that they had to do things the 'proper' way, the villagers warmed to them. Gemini and Henry Pesterdear became close friends and lunch-buddies, and even Edna mellowed. Puddlebrain remained quiet and unassuming and the 'baby'. Bless her.

The arguments had been there beforehand, and they were still there, only more pronounced and over even sillier things, afterwards. A cough, a sneeze, a thank you or please could set off a squabble that would send spiders and bats scurrying for cover as the air turned thick with curses. In fact, a murder of crows that had nested for many a year in the loft had packed up and left without so much as a goodbye note because they just couldn't take it anymore. Puddlebrain knew just how they felt. If she'd been tethered, she'd be at the end of it. But such was life in the witches' household. If you didn't like it, you were more than welcome to lump it.

At Halloween it was worse. Halloween was when a witch's powers were at their strongest. The problem was, you had to actually have powers in the first place. Edna, Gemini and Puddlebrain didn't. Each Halloween, they hoped something would somehow happen to return their magic. They didn't know what or how or why, but that didn't matter. Halloween was Witch Time. Surely *something* must happen? But it didn't. The three gathered around their cauldron each year, after Gemini had more or less (more rather than less) licked it clean, joined hands, and hoped. They hoped, wished, begged even, for whatever spirits that might be listening to take pity on their plight. It didn't work. By midnight the begging turned to bitching and the hoping to harping.

The Mayor would have been proud.

Once a vague mist had arisen from the cauldron causing the sisters to catch their breaths in anticipation, but it proved only to be a bit of untimely flatulence on the part of Gemini from consuming just a little too much spicy hogwort pie. Granted, flatulence from Gemini was untimely on any occasion, but that didn't seem to matter. Luckily she could run faster than Edna.

Amazingly, no one blamed Edna for their predicament. Well, they *blamed* her, but didn't come right out and slap her across the face with it, something they certainly felt like more often than not. They never spoke of the mishap again, at least after they were able to string a complete sentence together that didn't include the word 'Ribbit'. While they were still speaking in froggy language, they could have been saying anything.

So.

Gemini had whined about the soup and Puddlebrain had gone for a lie down. Edna was serving up, slopping the chicken and bladderwrack soup into large bowls. The rain was sleepily tapping against the window and the sky was sulking.

Chapter Five

If you left the sisters to their bumbling, went out the back garden gate, turned right and walked down the lane, you'd pass Mrs. Mead's on the left hand side. The bouncy, merry Mrs. Mead lived opposite Mrs. Burrows, who'd, most likely, be standing at her front door, shouting the comings and goings of the world back to Arthur, her husband. Arthur would, most likely, be fast asleep in his favourite chair, oblivious to his wife's barks. If you passed them by without a second look (or a third if you'd already taken a second), but ensuring you'd smelled the delightful aroma of merry Mrs. Mead's home baked sausage pie, you'd come to a crossroads.

Left would take you to the grand Town Hall and the bakery where merry Mrs. Mead sold her wares on a Wednesday afternoon, while the road right wound on aways, past the Miller's and the Bopsidy's until it came to the school. Quentin Bopsidy, third eldest son of a third eldest son, was Headmaster at the village school and, even though he lived only a hop, skip and a bumps-i-daisy away, he still managed to be late every morning. But that's by the bye and back again. Straight on from the only crossroads in the village, called The Crossroads for want of a more imaginative and less humdrum name, at the end of a road that had no twists or turns or even so much as a hiccup along its length, was the Field.

The Field was named such because that's what it was, much in the same way as The Crossroads was where two roads crossed. It was officially just out of town, a track that was more dirt than road separating it from the village boundary. A sign stood at the junction of road and track proclaiming:

Welcome to Little Whimsy
Population more than a few
Please drive your wagons carefully through our village.

It might come as a surprise that the village wasn't called simply The Village going on past experience, but it had a real goshdarnit name thanks to Mayor Pentonville, Mayor Harpy's eighty-ish times predecessor. Mayor Pentonville woke one morning from a dream he couldn't remember, and decided his village should have a name. The surrounding towns and villages had names, and so should his. His idea was met with a whole range of emotions, from disinterest to just plain not caring, so Little Whimsy finally stamped its footprint on the map. It had a manor house, a school and a crossroads. Not just a crossroads, but a *Crossroads.* Impressive, huh?

So, the Field. Children played, picnics were had and couples walked whispering and laughing and holding hands. At the far corner, just before the Field became Grimace Woods, was the Hill. The Hill was, amazingly, just that. A hill. It wasn't so small as to be called the Bump, nor was it by any means fair or foul the Mountain. It was somewhere in between, although it was definitely closer to Bump than Mountain. Grass grew freely about its surface and the occasional rabbit or fox would use it as a convenient sundeck to top up their tan on a hot day.

Behind the Hill, however, in the gasp between rise and wood, was the Hole.

The Hole was about two metres across and more or less round, or about as round as a five year old might be able to draw a circle with their eyes closed. It was also, roughly, forever deep. It hid, forgotten, behind the Hill, a vague memory in the dusty backrooms of the oldest villagers' heads (the oldest villagers being the witches). Lying, as it did, in the snatch of space between knoll and tree, it remained unseen and unthought of. If anyone were to look in that general direction, they'd simply see the Hill and Grimace Woods. As the woods were too dark and knotted to bear closer inspection – no one took their dogs for walks or climbed the trees – the Hole was content in its anonymity.

Just after thirteen o'clock a few days before Halloween, while Edna, Gemini and Puddlebrain were bimbling along, almost happy in their lives, a vague, greenish mist snaked out of the Hole. It hung for a second on the air, a slim tendril of nothing, and then dissipated, fading from view like steam on a mirror. There was a long pause, as if something deep, deep down was thinking, then the Hole belched. A cloud of the same greenish tinged mist shot up as if spat out like vomit from a kettlebird (which, strangely, wasn't a bird, but rather was a cow-like creature that had a nasty habit of eating holly, a leaf which just didn't agree with the poor animals digestive system).

Back at the house, Puddlebrain scratched her head, just behind her right ear. Gemini sneezed and Edna hiccupped. Gemini scraped the mucus from the top of her soup and carried on eating. Puddlebrain rolled over on her bed and closed her eyes. She began snoring softly a few minutes later.

Two doors down from Mrs. Mead lived Ethel Ribblesbottom. Ethel loved pets. She lived alone, and had done ever since her husband Terrence sadly passed away four years earlier. There was only her, an angelfish, three dogs, seventeen cats and a goat. As the Hole burped, two of the dogs hid under the bed, the third started chasing its tail and the seventeen cats all started mewing the tune to 'I'm a Sheckle and I'm Proud, Proud, Proud!'. Well, it probably wasn't quite that song, but it sounded almost as bad. Arthur Burrows woke up for the first time to hear something other than his wife going on and on and on and (and so on) while Mrs. Burrows found she couldn't actually speak at all.

And Puddlebrain had scratched her ear.

Chapter Six

The witches' house was settled at one end of Shadowmoss Lane. Apart from Windermere's place, a ramshackle old shed that looked like a good wind could blow it over (and many a good wind had tried), theirs was the only actual house on the lane. A couple of leftover shells that were cottages once, a long time before, and a good many vacant plots were all that filled the rest of the street. The witches didn't take it personally. It came with the territory – people didn't totally trust them no matter how nice they tried to be and how warm they were received. Seriously, Edna hadn't done any *real* damage with her magic and it was all in fun anyway. The rest of the time they tried their best to be helpful. Mostly, people treated them with courtesy, but no one would actually move in next to them.

Windermere was a special case. He was a right old grumpy gumdrop and was as set in his ways as an apple falling from a tree – it was going to go *down* no matter what anyone might think, want or care. Windermere, who might once have had a second name but seemed to have lost it along the way… unless Windermere actually *was* his second name, in which case he'd lost his first name, didn't take anyone's side except his own and wouldn't be run out of town by anyone, least of all witchin' folk. He was old and probably more infirm than the hovel he lived in, but he was staying put, and no young whippersnip was going to tell him otherwise, you hear?

Windermere could only walk with the aid of his crutches, of which he only really needed one, but used two because he didn't like odd numbers. He always slept on the right side of his bed and every chipped cup and cracked pot had to be lined up and straight with every dusty and dirty other thing in his kitchen. But, although his house was the next best thing to a pile of rubble, Windermere kept himself clean-shaven and spick. He'd keep himself span too if he could, but his age sometimes got the better of him and he couldn't always manage to be both spick *and* span. Halfway there was quite acceptable though.

He'd lived on Shadowmoss Lane for as long as he could remember and no amount of pressure from those villager types or mysteriousness stuff from the witchin' folk would force him out of his home, or at least shamble, or maybe shuffle, him out.

Between the two houses was a whole host of nothing. Windermere could see the witches' house from his front room, if the light was good and his eyes weren't playing him up, as they often did nowadays, but he didn't normally bother. He wasn't interested in the comings and going and wotnots of the rest of the world. He was content to simply be left alone in his grumpiness. The witches realised this and did just that. Besides, most of the time they simply forgot Windermere was even there.

In contrast to the run down state of the old man's house, Edna, Gemini and Puddlebrain's dwelling was both spick *and* span. They kept it clean themselves, with a great deal of help from the bewitched brooms and similar items. Though the witches had lost their magic many decades before, the house and its contents had kept on cleaning and opening and so on. The brooms, being unable to fly anymore, contented themselves with chasing dust about the floor. The grass in the well kept garden was allowed to grow how it pleased, but remained a respectful length, except for when Puddlebrain fancied a run in tall grass or a hunt through the jungle.

On these occasions, the grass would suddenly grow another few inches or, in the case of the jungle, a few feet. The path, as Mayor Harper discovered, led the way wherever the witches desired, and the pond, well populated by carp and trout aplenty, was a spring-fresh haven for all manner of insects. The pond, as with the path and the grass, followed the moods of the witches. It would be still as glass if Edna was on the warpath, or bubble a small fountain if Puddlebrain needed relaxing. The witches were the friends of their surroundings, and their surroundings were friends back.

Well, apart from that gnome out back.

A door from the kitchen led out onto a small patio area in the back garden. To one side (the left, to be precise) was a slight dip that, over the centuries, had become a hollow. In the middle of the hollow, due partly to an accident Gemini had once had when she fancied orange grass instead of green, was a scorched patch of bare earth. In the centre of the scorched patch lived a gnome called Billy.

Billy the gnome was an exile. He'd been cast out of Templemead, the gnome capital city far off to the east, for not being sneaky enough. He could never quite get the knack of tricking people out of their belongings and his pranks didn't have the decency to work out. They always backfired on him - literally sometimes - and so he just couldn't live up to the ideal of being a gnome. If his nose was a little more crooked and his back was a touch more humped, he could maybe pass for a goblin, but the gnome race had pretty much turned its collective back on him.

He had wandered for months with his resentment swirling and bubbling like a cauldron of Edna's bladderwrack soup and had finally decided to take his revenge on the witches. He had no real reason to other than he just happened to be passing. It was their fault they put their house right where he wanted to walk, so they would pay for it, and they could also pay for the attitude of his fellow gnomes into the bargain. Billy was generous like that. Why cause a lot of people bother when you could lump it all on one person, or three in this case. He plonked his bum in the nice, comfy patch of black bristle that had once been grass and proceeded to hurl abuse at the witches every time they happened to poke their heads out of their back door.

Billy had been out there for around four years. He'd curse and swear and try, unsuccessfully, to play practical jokes on the sisters. The thing was, they quite liked him, in a sort of repulsed kind of way. He provided a welcome distraction from their own problems and, regardless of his attitude towards them, they thought he might be… fond was perhaps too strong a word… let's just say Billy might not dislike them as much as he made out. The cold and stale leftovers they threw at him on an almost daily basis were about the only kindness the gnome had ever been shown in his wretched life. It wasn't every day, of course. They didn't want him getting any ideas.

Gnomes made a distinct effort to *not* be kind. Sympathy and gentleness were disgusting to the gnarled little creatures, so much so that they didn't even have words for such *nice* qualities. *Ugh.* A gnome would rather cut off his own head than show consideration to another, and some had even done so when they'd been caring accidentally.

So, being a gnome, the witches' kindness was a great big fat no-no to him. Even though he appreciated it way on down deep inside, he had to show his rage, so the tirade continued, sometimes, for hours and often long into the night. They needed to be shown, those witches, and Billy was just the gnome to do it!

Of course, while he was showing them, he'd just stay where he was, comfy in the bristle patch, taking their food. Just to make sure they learned their lesson, you understand.

Chapter Seven

Edna, Gemini and Puddlebrain had lived in the house since they were born. Their parents had lived in it for most of their extremely long, even by witch standards, lives before that. It hadn't changed much in all those centuries, the sisters preferring to leave it just as their parents had liked. Magic could come in very useful occasionally so they had made some of the rooms a little bigger, and had extended the kitchen to include a pantry and washroom. Otherwise it was much the same dwelling that Corinne and Colin had occupied for so long. Oh, the garden did look after itself now. Colin, the sisters' father, had been a keen gardener and liked little more than getting his hands dirty tending his plot. None of the daughters had any horticultural tendencies, so left it to magic to keep things neat. The house was simple – three bedrooms, a living room with a huge open fire, the kitchen, a bathroom and a cupboardy thing under the stairs that no one could quite figure out what to do with. Apart from a couple of hidey-holes for shoving junk and stuff in, that was your lot. It suited them right down to the ground and back again. It was home.

By an obnoxious mix of bad luck and misfortune, Puddlebrain's room was at the back, directly over where Billy the gnome was encamped. She had the displeasure of having to listen to him rant endlessly while she was struggling to invent new ways to get to sleep. Hers was the 'box' room, so called because it wasn't much larger than one and you'd be hard pushed to swing the proverbial cat, not that Puddlebrain would ever consider doing anything like that. The word 'room' was entirely misleading, as it implied that there was actually some.

Room, that is. In Puddlebrain's case there was space for a bed and a wardrobe and a small cramped table.

Edna's and Gemini's rooms were palatial in contrast. Their bedrooms were twice the size of their younger sister's, and you could swing a donkey if you fancied it. Their extravagance was squandered though, as they had the same furniture as Puddlebrain. In each room lived a bed, a wardrobe and a small cramped table. Such a waste.

The living room was only a little larger than Puddlebrain's bedroom. There was a wide sofa facing the fire and a low table, stained and chipped from decades of misuse and neglect. There was no real point in having any more furniture as the fireplace dominated the entire room, making any other adornments redundant. It had an ornate oak surround, carved in a single piece by their father, and was cut from the biggest of the three oaks that pretty much owned the centre of Grimace Woods. He'd ventured in on only one occasion, with the express desire to create this fire surround, but had never braved its confines again. He declined to ever speak of what he found within the Grimace, saying only that it was 'quiet'.

The surround was sculpted with the likenesses of myriad faerie creatures, each of which grabbed your attention in turn by smiling, waving or, on occasion, even singing to you. The fireplace itself led through to the kitchen on the other side, but it was never a thoroughfare as a roaring log fire always raged in its grate, even in the hottest summer. There was no chimney leading up through the roof to swallow the smoke as the fire burned cleanly, emitting only the odd spark and crackle just to say 'Hi there! Warm enough for ya?'

In each room, windows, large and clear, looked onto the outside world, allowing no one to look back in. From that there outside world, the house looked like it was in perpetual darkness, as if the sun had forgotten to rise and the day had overslept and not got round to breaking. It was an illusion, however. Even on the most overcast and gloomy day, the inside of the witches' home was summer-bright.

The sisters had lived there all their lives and couldn't imagine living anywhere else. In fact, they couldn't imagine imagining it. It was home. They did their best to look after it, which wasn't too easy when you had lost your magic and weren't too well practiced with polishing a floor, and the house looked after them in turn.

But when the Hole belched and Gemini sneezed, when Edna hiccupped and Puddlebrain scratched her ear, a little patch of darkness started to slowly spread in the furthest corner under Puddlebrain's bed, just below where her head was gently snoring. It wasn't quite black – it was more like a vague shadow that you could only see if you looked sideways on with your eyes squinty. Even then you'd be hard pushed to convince yourself that it wasn't just your imagination playing tricks on you like Billy the gnome tried to but couldn't.

Chapter Eight

Quentin Bopsidy was late. It was Wednesday morning, the day after the night before, and he was late.

How could this be? He lived not a Lig's leap from the school, yet he still managed to end up running up the front path, crunching the gravel and struggling not to slip if it had been raining (or even if it had not), desperate to be there for morning assembly. He was late, full stop and that be the end of it. Even Old Missus Wigan, the cleaner, bless her little woolly socks, managed to beat him to his office on a daily basis. That wouldn't have been so bad, but she couldn't walk more than two steps an hour or so and constantly had to ask passers-by directions because "My eyesight isn't what it used to be, dearie."

Old Missus Wigan, whose skin was like parchment and whose voice was the same, was only really still employed because no one had the heart to let her go. She didn't want to be put out to pasture like a sad old horse that couldn't pull the plough all around the field anymore. The fact was, even though everyone thought her name really was 'Old Missus Wigan', she did manage to pull that plough all around the field, or in this case, the mop around the school. It took her a while to do so, but by the end of the day, the school was as spotless as Mrs. Mead's stove. Proud of that stove, was merry Mrs. Mead. Couldn't be baking on a mucky-yucky stove, no way no how.

The bell had gone before Quentin had even opened his bleary eyes. The bell, a great brass instrument that could be heard all over Little Whimsy if it was given enough welly, should have been donged by the headmaster himself. The task had been passed onto Prefect Benjamin Waddle, top of his class in every class and the only boy who was big enough to heft the thing. He was also the only pupil who got to school early enough to ring it. Prefect Benjamin, top of each of his classes and punctual as a nine-penny piece, was early to everything. He'd been a week early to his birth and his dad, William Waddle the gardener ("Cut and sow, trim and mow, I'm the man to make your garden grow!"), said he'd chance be early to his own funeral. It was his donging of the bell's ding that woke up the headmaster, and not for the first time.

Three times a week, at least that was the usual count. The pupils ran a little bet as to how many times Mr. Bopsidy would be late, the winner getting sweets for a week. It had been Fenella Caroline, daughter of Arthur Burrows' second cousin, a very unsavoury character by the name of Brian, who had won the past two weeks. Brian Caroline was well known as a scoundrel and a layabout, but Fenella was quite the opposite. She was cheerful and polite and as friendly as they came. She had guessed correctly that Quentin would be late four times last week and four times the week before. Her school satchel was fair bursting at the seams with chocolates and boiled sweets.

Quentin rubbed his eyes wearily. He yawned and stretched, his joints cracking in protest. He scratched his head, sleepily sure there was something he had to do. He crawled out of bed and shambled into the bathroom. As was usual for the headmaster, he scribbled his fingers through his wild hair – his version of brushing it – and splashed his face with cold water. He stared at his reflection in the mirror, pulling at the skin on his face, vainly hoping that he could perhaps stretch the wrinkles out, and then shambled back into the bedroom. Just another five minutes. He had crawled back into bed, pulling the covers up to his neck, when he realised what, exactly, he had to do.

Headmaster. That was it. School.

LATE!

Ah.

He threw the covers off and leaped back out of bed. He stood, swaying, his head swimming. Bad idea, jumping up like that. Your head didn't have chance to keep up. Once his brain had settled back into his head, Quentin grabbed his clothes and dragged them on. He scrambled about for a matching pair of clean socks, and pulled on a mismatched pair of one black and one stripy green when he couldn't find any. He glanced in the long mirror that hung on the far bedroom wall, not really seeing himself. He just barely registered that he, at least, wasn't going to walk out of the house with his jumper on back to front or with no trousers. Then he ran to the front door.

Quentin Bopsidy was what some might call a beanpole. That description was close, but it lacked something – not least that no one really knew just what a beanpole looked like. He was more like a few bamboo shoots thrown together. His body and arms were long, gangly stretches with knobbly bits along the way for his hips, ankles and wrists and his head was like a big peanut balancing precariously on top. His hair was an insane mix of grey, black and orange as if someone had dropped a tin of paint on his head when he was a baby, and it had never washed out. He didn't run, he loped. His long legs extended out, making him look like a scarecrow that had been scared by a murder of crows. He slammed the front door on his way out and pelted up the path towards the school, almost tripping over Marilyn the moggie, one of Ethel Ribblesbottom's cats, in his haste.

Somewhere between Marilyn the moggie and the school gates, something happened.

Quentin never made it to school that day.

There was no kafuffle. There was no noise or anything so notable. Simply, Quentin Bopsidy, headmaster and Captain of the Unpunctuality team (or he would be if there was one), didn't arrive to take morning assembly. He had still not turned up to take afternoon register. The only witness to what really happened was Marilyn the moggie who, quite frankly, had seen better days and who, whoever Frank was, couldn't see much of anything anyway.

By mid-afternoon, it was obvious something had happened to the headmaster. Granted he was rarely on time, but he at least always managed to get there in the end. Mr. Cowling, the arithmetic teacher who hated to be called the maths teacher, spent three quarters of an hour knocking alternatively on Quentin's front door, back door and windows. There was no sign of him.

By three o'clock, almost everyone in Little Whimsy knew that he'd disappeared. On the other side of the town hall from the bakery, was the Tea Shop, owned for many years by Edward Corrigan and his dear wife Brenda. It served tea, buttered scones and three kinds of gossip at very reasonable prices. On this occasion, it was having one of its busiest days ever. It was as if the local constabulary had moved offices into the tea shop as what could easily have been an incident room had been set up. Brenda was holding court while Edward kept the tea flowing and the scones buttered. There was standing room only and not a lot of that.

The fact that they were discussing Quentin Bopsidy was really a mere side issue. Certainly the residents of Little Whimsy were concerned about the headmaster, but come *on* people! Juicy gossip like this didn't come along very often so when it did, you grabbed it by the horns, gave it a good yank and sank your teeth in deep!

"Doesn't he have a sister over in Harpston?" asked Pole. Pole was a short stumpy man who only shaved once a month and then only because he got fed up of his wife's moaning about the fact that his whiskers tickled. "Maybe he's just gone visiting."

Brenda stared at Pole as if she'd been slapped. How dare he have a reasonable explanation for something like this! The idea that the headmaster had just climbed aboard the inter-village wagon and had taken himself off for a few days was unthinkable!

"Pole, dear," she said in an even voice. "Quentin's *cousin* lives in Harpston, and they haven't spoken in three years. Please check your facts before jumping in."

Pole bit his tongue. He couldn't see that facts had much to do with anything in this situation. They were more of an inconvenience. And he knew it was Quentin's sister living in Harpston, not his cousin. His cousin lived in Wilma, aways over the other side of Townston. And the reason he hadn't spoken to her for three years was because it took a week to get there by wagon and he couldn't be away from school for too long, and his cousin couldn't read, so there was no point in writing. He knew this because he and Quentin played kickball together on a Friday night.

So there.

"Now," said Brenda. She raised her voice a little to make sure she could be heard, but she didn't need to. Everyone in the room was listening intently. "Do we have any *constructive* ideas?"

"Maybe he was eaten by wolves," said Lem Artthorpe (that's *two* T's, thank you very much). "What if they dragged him into his garden and chewed him to pieces? Maybe we should dig up his garden to be sure!"

A bustle of oohs and aahs and gasps was quickly followed by half the men in the tea shop rising to their feet, ready to grab shovels and uproot the headmaster's extremely well-kept garden. Brenda cleared her throat and the bustle died to a few anxious whispers.

"Lemon Artthorpe! Do you *have* to?" Brenda eyed him sternly. "You remember that word I taught you? Tact?"

Lem was usually about as tactful as a brick. He didn't see the point in soft soaping hard edges 'cos, he reckoned, you'd get cut all the same.

"Well, you all want something bad to happen to him anyways," Lem insisted. "You want to rub your hands and mop your teary eyes and say what a nice man he was. If he turned up tomorrow having drunk one too many pints of ale, you'd all feel hard done by."

The truth, more often than not, hurts. It did in this instance, so Brenda gave Lemon a quick cuff about the ear.

"You mind your ways, Lemon Artthorpe. Time was we had to go looking for you. Time was *you'd* had one too many pints of ale yourself. Time was, if we hadn't been woritin ourselves over your sorry hide, you'd probably still be asleep under that fallen willow. So you just mind, 'kay?"

Lem looked sheepishly at the floor, avoiding the smirks and giggles.

Could've been wolves, he thought. *Could've been.*

Not everyone was laughing at Lem, though. One or two, like Arthur Burrows and Brian Mead, Mrs. Mead's husband, were still thinking about the wolves. Granted, wolves hadn't been seen hereabouts for a good many years, but that didn't mean there wasn't any coal in the bunker, and a great big pile of it at that!

Wendy Plumrose stood up. She was young and pretty and never really thought anything through. Her sister Julia was also young and pretty, but she thought everything through, often not getting round to doing things because she was still deep in thought two days after whatever thing it was had needed to be done.

"I heard," she said, speaking as if she was addressing the Town Council (most of whom where here anyway), "that he was carrying on with…"

A tumble of grumbles drowned out the rest of her sentence. Wendy thought that everyone was carrying on with everyone else, except who they were meant to be carrying on with, so much so that she frequently managed to tangle herself up in the web of him-and-her-and-they-and-ohdidyousee that she'd created. As soon as she started off on one of her infamous scandals, pretty much everyone remembered something else they had to be doing, even if they didn't have anything else to do.

Brenda held up her hand to calm the hubbub.

"Does anyone else have anything to add?"

A small, crinkly man at the back stood up. Ingle Faltering was not everyone's idea of an ideal citizen. In fact, Fenella Caroline's father was almost a prince in comparison. He wasn't tolerated, as Mr. Caroline was, he was just ignored. People were so used to turning their noses up at him and pretending he wasn't there, they often really did forget he was there.

His voice was as crumpled as his appearance, but it had an underlying slimy texture that, if he said anything within earshot, made you want to wipe your hands because they felt dirty.

"What about the witches?"

Chapter Nine

A hush fell on the crowded room as if either Brenda had held up her hand, which she had not, or someone had stuffed the occupants' mouths with cotton wool, which they hadn't either. Everyone looked guiltily at everyone else.

"That's what I thought," said Brenda. That was the straw that broke the dam, unleashing a cacophony of shouts and yells, all with one thing in common.

The witches.

Suddenly, it was what everyone had thought but, for some reason, no one had wanted to say. Ignoring the fact that it was widely known that they'd lost their powers many years before, it had to be them. Disregarding the way people actually, mostly, liked the witches, it simply *had* to be them!

The tea room went through a strange metamorphosis then. It changed from an incident room concerning the disappearance of a headmaster into a war office with the sole intent of making some witches disappear. Some people even went so far as attempting to smash tables so they could use the legs as stakes.

"Stake through the heart. It's the only way."

Brenda put a stop to those shenanigans.

"Touch my furniture and you won't have to worry about the witches. You'll have to worry about me. And it's vampires, not witches. With witches, you burn them at the stake, not put one through their hearts."

That was all that was needed. The tea room emptied in seconds and a mob of angry villagers, excited and enraged in complete contrast to their usual demeanour of not really caring about much in general, set on a stampede aimed directly at the far end of Shadowmoss Lane. A handful of men broke off from the pack to start erecting a podium in the centre of the Town Square. Hardly a coherent word was spoken that could be heard above the rabble, yet everyone was moving as if with one mind.

The Square was a serene place normally. It was beautifully landscaped with wooden benches set out randomly. The horde tore up the benches and uprooted shrubs and bushes, kicking, throwing and snapping them. The larger pieces were lashed together to create the post. The smaller scraps of wood were strewn about its base for the kindling. By the time it was done, the rest of the crowd had reached Shadowmoss Lane and were descending on the sisters' home.

Windermere peered out from his dusky front room, aroused from his afternoon kip by the noise. He peered out of his grimy windows and shook his head. It had to happen, he thought. Sooner or later. He didn't want to witness the inevitable, so he turned and shuffled back to bed.

The mob stopped at the garden gate in a scene that strangely mirrored a certain Mayor decades before. They looked at each other, their heads whipping about like rabid dogs, waiting for someone to take control. Naturally, it was Brenda. She pushed open the gate and strode forward. The path thought briefly about guiding her back to where she started, but thought better of it. It realised nothing so simple would stop the raging madwoman.

A rational thought managed to struggle to the surface in the mind of not-so-merry Mrs. Mead. "What if they, you know, *do* something to you?"

Mrs. Mead no longer cared that she and Edna shared the same love for teapot collecting. Brenda happily chatted to all three sisters on their frequent visits to her shop. She knew Edna and Gemini took two sugars in their tea but Puddlebrain took none because, bless her, she was sweet enough. Well, that sweetness left a distinctly bitter taste in her mouth now. She wished she had said that thought out loud. It was witty and sharp and nasty enough to be proud of. Oh well. She filed it away. Maybe she could use it later and impress the jury as the witches burned.

"They wouldn't dare!" she hissed.

Inside the house...

"I am not chewing your toenails!" shouted Puddlebrain. "Last time, you still had fluff in them from those stupid stripy socks you always wear!"

"My stripy socks are *not* stupid!" Gemini shouted back. "They just didn't have a very good education. It isn't their fault. They can't help it if..."

"What are you on about?" Puddlebrain clenched her fists by her side. *Oh for a spell right now!*

"You were having a go at my poor socks! That's not fair. I only asked if you'd trim my toenails for me."

Puddlebrain made a strangled *uurrrrghhhh* sound and went to storm off to her room. She was interrupted by a harsh rapping at the front door.

"Who's that?"

"Well, if we still had our magic, I might be able to tell you," Edna sneered. "But as we don't, *why don't you answer it!*"

Puddlebrain thought briefly about commenting on their lack of magic, and why exactly they had a lack of magic, but the banging on the door was repeated.

"Why don't you!" she snapped.

"You!"

"No, you!"

"Oh, I'll answer it!" Gemini shouted above the rapidly rising noise. She stood and stomped over to the door, yanking it open. "Yes?"

Outside the house Brenda had heard the muffled yells from within. Though she wasn't the arrogant fool Mayor Harper had been so many years previously, she was still so full of herself she was fit to burst at the seams. She quaked a little at the prospect of the witches being angry, and the possibility of that anger being directed at her, but it was only a little. She was she, and woe betide any who might forget that little fact.

OK, so she was as arrogant as Mayor Plumptious, but he was her grandfather on her mother's side, so perhaps that explained things a little.

When Gemini snatched the door open it took Brenda by surprise. Granted, she had been knocking, somewhat vigorously, on it at the time, but it still made her gasp. When Gemini's plump little head appeared, right in her face, she took an involuntary step back.

"Oh," said Gemini. "It's you. Sorry about that. How are you?"

Brenda frowned. Surely the witches wouldn't be so calm and friendly if they had really taken Mr. Bopsidy? They'd be hiding behind twitching curtains or come out with fingers a-blazing. They wouldn't just say 'Hi.'

Ah, but what if that was what they wanted you to think? What if they knew you'd figure that so did the opposite to put you off the smell. Clever. Sneaky. Well she wouldn't fall for that old one. The smell stunk as far as she was concerned. She'd show them. Play it cool. That was the way.

"Grab 'em!" she yelled.

Chapter Ten

The mob at the gate had been waiting for a signal of some kind, but had thought it would be something subtle; a cough or a wave meant to take the witches unawares. There was a fraction of a second's pause while it sank in just what Brenda had meant, then they stormed the house, makeshift weapons held high and shouts held even higher. The fence didn't really stand a chance and became the first casualty of war with the silverfish barely escaping being the second. They crashed through the garden, trampling everything in their path and pushed into the house, carrying Brenda along with them. Gemini stumbled back, stunned, and fell against her sisters. Before any of them could speak, they had been bound, gagged and hooded to prevent them using any of their accursed powers.

When the hoods were removed, the three sisters found themselves in the Town Square, tied securely to the stake. Around them, standing silently, almost fearful, were the villagers. None could look the witches in the eye as they guiltily shuffled about, their faces downward. Only Brenda held her head up.

"So, witches," she shouted, even though everyone could hear her. "What have you done with him?"

The sisters looked at each other. What on earth was happening? Was this some kind of Halloween prank? But Halloween was still days away, and it wasn't very funny. These were their friends. Edna had swapped teapots with Brenda Corrigan. They looked around them and saw what was obviously kindling, and a lot of it, stacked at their feet. It didn't take a genius to figure out what was going on. Gemini was a buttered bap short of the whole buffet, but even she realised, with a choked gasp, what was happening. Witches hadn't been burned at the stake for hundreds of years! This was *insane*!

Brenda took their silence to mean the obvious, or at least the obvious from where she was standing, which was as far from the witches as she could stand without appearing afraid.

"Tell us," she said, "and we'll make this as painless as possible. Keep silent and I won't be responsible for what might happen."

This was true. Brenda certainly wouldn't be the one to light the match, that was for sure. She had flunkies for that. Her husband for one.

Edna, eldest of the sisters, was automatically the one they looked to for help. Even given their predicament, she was still the same Edna that had faced down the Mayor decades before. It was one of the reasons she and her current adversary got on so well. They were strong women who stood up for what they believed in, in some cases regardless of whether or not they were right.

"Brenda Corrigan, what *is* going on?"

That old act-as-if-you-don't-know trick. It wasn't going to work, so they may as well drop it.

"Don't act as if you don't know, *witch!* What have you done with him?"

"Who? What are you rambling on about woman?"

Brenda took great offence at anyone who implied she might ramble. As far as she was concerned, she spoke her mind, got right to the point, didn't waffle, just bang, straight and true. Anyone who got in the way should beware. Her tongue was sharper than any old knife as Edward, her carefully devoted husband, had learned very early on in their marriage. She took a deep breath and, through teeth clamped tighter than her father's wallet, the mean old duffer, she said…

… not a word.

Without a flash or a fart, Brenda Corrigan was *gone.* In mid-taunt, she was no longer mid-anything. A vague cloud of green that made you think your eyes were a little out of focus and you should maybe visit the optician over in Hathaway, which was over thataway but wasn't really worth the wagon ride, hung for a second in the air before fading, the world coming once more into a stark clarity.

Gemini and Puddlebrain stared at Edna in amazement and she stared back at them. She shook her head. She was sure she hadn't… didn't… *couldn't…* had she?

The hungry pack that had been so eager to satiate their thirst for vengeance stood for in stunned silence. Their heads swung from where their unofficial leader had been standing to the witch, moving back and forth like cats hypnotised by a moving light. A yelp from somewhere near the back broke the spell they couldn't have been under, because the witches were sure they'd lost their magic, and they suddenly fled. The Town Square emptied in seconds, leaving the three witches tied to the stake.

Gemini and Puddlebrain continued to stare at their sister. It was a cool trick, but why didn't she tell them she had her powers back? Edna could see what they were thinking, but she *hadn't!* She *couldn't!*

Could she? Edna concentrated hard on the ropes that held their hands tight behind them. She took a deep breath and moved her finger in a small circular motion. Nothing happened. She tried again, making the circle bigger. Still nothing.

"It wasn't me," she said quietly. For a second, she thought it might have been. She thought maybe, somehow, their magic had returned. It hadn't. "It wasn't me," she repeated.

"Well if it wasn't you, then who was it? Know any other witches hanging around?" asked Gemini. "Come on Edna. Tell all. How long have you known?"

"I don't know anything. I'm telling you it wasn't me!"

"Oh, come on. Why don't you just…?"

"I don't think it was her, Gemini," Puddlebrain interrupted. "We're sisters. If Edna had her magic back, then wouldn't we all? Besides, as nice as it is to get rid of that interfering busybody Brenda Corrigan, it was hardly the right way to do it, with a mob after our blood."

Gemini shut up. Puddlebrain had a point, but if it wasn't Edna, then who?

"We won't find anything out stuck up here. We need to get down. Do either of you have any scissors or a knife?" Edna asked.

"Oh yes," said Gemini sarcastically. "I have both in my pocket! Which would you prefer? I've got a hammer and nails in my other pocket so we can rebuild the benches while we're at it!"

"No, Edna," said Puddlebrain. "We don't. Face it, we can't get out."

"Don't be daft. You think a few bits of string are going to hold me down? Never in a month of Wednesday afternoons."

Edna took a deep breath, then tried to force her arms apart. When it, surprisingly, didn't snap the thick ropes that bound them, she tried wriggling about to loosen them. When that didn't work, she turned to the others.

"Well don't just stand there!" she snapped. "Help me! I can't do this on my own!"

Gemini joined her in her wriggles and squirms. Puddlebrain simply watched them for a few moments.

"It's not going to work. They're too tight and too thick. Maybe one of the villagers will come back and let us out," she said.

"And pigs might dance the tango!" Edna shouted. "Get a grip, Puddlebrain. If they come back, it'll be to cook us good and proper, with nary a roast spud or cauliflower floret in sight. We are on our own!"

"Oh, I wouldn't be saying that," said a voice. "I wouldn't be saying that at all."

Chapter Eleven

All three witches turned towards the voice. They recognised it instantly. It had been taunting them for the past four years.

"Billy!" they cried together.

"What are you doing here?" said Puddlebrain excitedly.

"What do you think? I've come to save you useless ninnies. Think I'm going to let you get away with someone else punishing you? Not a chance. Besides, I'm hungry, and it's about time you threw me some of that slop you call food."

"Oh, bless you, Billy!" Edna said. "You can have all the slop you ever want!"

"Oh, don't be getting all fussy and all with me. And don't be offering me a whole swill of that so-called food. You want to make me sick? Just a few bits here and there are all I can stomach, so we'll leave it at that. You hear?"

"Anything you say, Billy. Anything at all." Naturally she knew he loved the food they gave him, and was certain he'd scoff any amount they tossed his way and complain with every mouthful. But that was Billy the Gnome. That was why they liked him. Besides, none of them were going to argue with the only person who would help them.

"Right," said the gnome. "Let's get you out of there before those knuckle heads come back. Don't want me being charcoal along with you lot."

Billy pulled a knife from under his tunic. It seemed too long for his small frame, but he held it comfortably as he scrambled over the wood surrounding the stake. Even though it shifted under his weight, he was sure-footed and in an instant was standing next to the witches.

"Now, I don't want you thanking me for none of this. I'm just thinking of myself here. Got that?"

"Got it," said Puddlebrain.

With a flick that was almost too fast to see, Billy cut the ropes that held the witches against the stake. Another couple of flicks severed the cords that bound their hands and feet. The sisters, once they had climbed down to more solid ground, rubbed their wrists and stamped their feet to get the feeling back. Gemini went to hug the gnome but he held his knife up in warning.

"We'll not have any of that foolishness," he snarled.

"Oh yes. Sorry." Gemini backed away.

"How did you know what was happening?" asked Edna.

"Yes," added Gemini. "And why did you help us? I thought you didn't like us."

"Well, I don't have any feelings either way, truth be told. As for the why-fore of it all, I've already explained myself there," said Billy, sliding his long knife back under his tunic. "As for the how-fore of it, I don't have ears like this for nowt!" He pulled on his large ears, stuck to the side his head like teacups – the big china ones that Brenda served her best tea to her best customers in. "Your welcoming party was making enough noise to wake a mish-mish bairn!"

The mish-mish was a small tribe of creatures vaguely resembling people with a little lizard thrown in for good measure. They lived in the mountains beyond the Aren Rush, a river that was so long it 'fair split the world in two' as some claimed. They had a thick coating of fur, which was shed during the three weeks of summer which blessed their mountain habitat. The mish-mish kept themselves to themselves and rarely ventured far from home, although many visitors passed through their village buying the coats and other knick-knacks woven from their discarded hair.

The mish-mish children had the unpleasant habit of crying constantly. Their voices were shrill and piercing and penetrated the thickest of earmuffs, causing the parents to take extreme measures to 'help' their young sleep. It meant they had developed extremely tough skulls, but the children certainly slept well.

"Anyway," said Billy. "We want to be getting our little butt-butts out of here unless you'd like to be first course on a barbecue menu. No telling when that lot will dare to come crawling back."

"He's right," said Edna. "We need to move."

"But where do we go?" asked Gemini. "We can't go home. They'll just come and drag us back here. We don't even know what we're supposed to have done!"

"Old Bopsidy the headmaster has gone and disappeared himself, that's what. They all think you've magicked him away somewhere, although why you'd waste your time with a fool like that, I don't know." Billy shook his head. "I'm surprised he was even on time for his own abduction."

"Quentin has disappeared?" gasped Puddlebrain. "What? Like Brenda did just then?"

"Well, not being there when it happened, I can hardly comment, now can I? But I'd hazard a decidedly non-hazardous guess that that'd be the case. Someone not in their right mind decided to take him off somewhere, and now they've done the self same thing to the old Corrigan woman. Give 'em a medal, I say."

"How do you know so much about all this, Billy?" asked Puddlebrain. "You spend all your time insulting us through our kitchen window."

"Oh, that's what I like to make you think," the gnome grinned. "I still like to know what's going on where I'm living, however grotty. Better to be prepared, don't you know." He leaned forward on tiptoes, almost managing to be nose to nose with Puddlebrain – close enough for his hot breath to make her nose want to shrivel up and hide in a corner. "But I think we'd better be discussing all this somewhere else, don't you?"

"But where?" asked Puddlebrain.

"Well, if I was you I'd be thinking like this," said the gnome. "That lot would probably expect you to stay well away from your home so that's the best place to go!"

Edna shook her head. "They're not all as daft as Peregrin, so they'd probably realise we'd think that and go there anyway."

Peregrin. A poor young lad who had never got anything right in his life. He, sadly, didn't make it past his teenage years due to an accident involving a cheese making machine and a bucket of milk. He was one of those boys who you just shook your head at because saying anything was pointless – he'd still be looking the other way when the postal wagon came down the street and he'd still forget that stepping stones were always wet and simply didn't like him and his balance was never that good anyway. Hence, he walked with a permanent limp and whistled when he talked thanks to his missing four front teeth. He was the prime example of ultimate daftness and his memorial was to forever be mentioned with regard to others of the same breed.

"There's no point in second guessing when you don't know the first guess," said Puddlebrain. "Billy is right. We should go home and quickly."

Edna and Gemini stared at her. They were not used to their baby sister being so assertive. Bless her. Billy broke the moment with an irritated "*Now?*"

The sisters and their gnome set off. They took a long, roundabout route home, expecting to encounter trouble at every turn. They passed, at one point, close to the Bopsidy house. Puddlebrain paused.

"Do you hear that?" she whispered, her head cocked to one side.

"What?" hissed Edna. They didn't have time to stop. "Is it the villagers?"

Puddlebrain frowned. She wasn't sure what she could hear, or even if she could hear anything at all. It was like an echo of a sound that hadn't really been noticed. She shook her head.

"Doesn't matter," she said. "Let's go."

Their next turn brought them to the Milch Mire, a completely unappetising bog that was not quite swamp but was well past muddy puddle. It wasn't big but it was messy and smelly, and unfortunately necessary. If they tried to go around it, valuable time would be wasted, and they risked being caught. There was no option. Billy took up a position on Puddlebrain's shoulders to avoid sinking without a trace. The Mire wasn't exactly deep, but even a puddle could be too much for a gnome. The witches trudged through it as quickly as they could, trying not to notice the rancid smells and obnoxious sounds that were released as the surface bubbled like a festering sore. Thankfully, just beyond the bog was Avril Wendie's back garden with its enormous pond, home to a few dozen carp.

The witches knew Wendie had been at the Town Square so took the risk of washing their feet in the pond. The rest of them would have to wait but they didn't want telltale footprints smudging the way to their house. A few more streets and it was only a hop, skip and a mad dash to their back gate. Once back home, they locked the doors, front and back, and requested politely that the doors stayed that way. Whether or not they would be strong enough to withstand a raging mob was unknown, but the witches were at least confident the doors would try their best. When that was done, they huddled down in the cellar.

Chapter Twelve

The cellar was a long low room. Well, it was more half a room – the bottom half. It was impossible for anyone (except perhaps Billy) to stand upright without scooping a hole out of the ceiling and having your head used as an ornamental coffee table in the room above. It was mostly bare apart from a few boxes and bags containing a collection of long forgotten heirlooms and junk. The cellar wasn't filthy, but nor was it as tidy as the rest of the house. Edna had decided that cellars are just meant to be dusty. It was in their nature. They wouldn't feel right without a nice layer of grit to clog your nostrils. The cellar was only too eager to agree and fulfilled the ideal admirably.

"What now?" asked Puddlebrain after the obligatory sneezing had subsided. She was crouched to one side, away from the door. Edna and Gemini had claimed the only two stools in the room so she had to resort to squatting. It felt very unladylike, but Puddlebrain had never been one to worry about being mistaken for a lady. She left that to Edna. Anyway, now was not the time to worry about such trivialities.

Edna was sitting opposite her youngest sister. It normally fell to her to come up with 'the plan' or make 'the decision'. Unfortunately, she had only had to face annoyance and frustration from the odd villager before. This mass hysteria was entirely new to her. The inhabitants of Little Whimsy had never bothered to bother with anything before. She didn't know what to say.

Gemini was perched on the edge of her stool, rocking backwards and forwards, humming softly to herself. She often did this, singing tuneless songs, when she was trying not to think of something. Except this time it wasn't working. She was worried verging on frantic and was desperately hoping Edna would come up with something to make things better. She liked better. It tasted nicer than the sour flavour of the cellar's dusty air.

The trio sat in silence, staring at the floor in the centre of the cellar, each waiting for the other to speak. Well, Gemini was waiting for supper too.

"Well," said Billy finally.

He stepped into the triangle of so-called witches and stood with his hands on his hips, his head cocked to one side. It was a pose full of sarcasm and derision and any other time Edna would swipe him across the back of his head for his insolence. Now, she simply looked at him, not even noticing his stance.

"This is a fine to-do, ain't it?" he scowled. "Three all-mighty witches reduced to hiding in their cellar for something they haven't even done. If there was a prize for the most unfortunate unfortunates, I reckon you'd be giving your acceptance speeches right about now. I'd like to thank my mother and father, but most of all you lovely people for hunting me down."

Edna frowned.

"What are you talking about? Shut up!"

They didn't need this. The gnome had helped them, granted. More than that, he'd saved them. But they didn't deserve this.

"Shut up? *Shut up?* Is that the best you can do?" Billy stepped forward, a little leap that got right up Edna's nose, along with a kick-full of dust. She coughed, he taunted. "Oh powerful one," he whined, "please don't hurt me. Please don't smite me down with your wicked words."

He sprang back to the middle and turned his attentions to Gemini.

"You going to sing something to tap our tired feet to there?" he said. "You going to get some *rhythm* going? Go on, you sing and I'll dance. Let's have a party!"

Gemini came out of her daze long enough to tell Billy to "*Shut up!*" before sinking back within herself.

"Shut up! Shut up!" whimpered Billy as he turned to Puddlebrain. "Oh so *scary*! What can you come up with?" he asked her. "Can the baby scream louder than the big 'uns? Or do you want to slink into a corner and suck your thumb? Boo-boo ga-ga bib-bib-bib?"

He reached up and tweaked Puddlebrain's cheeks. She slapped his hand away.

"Shut up," she mumbled.

"Shut up! Shut up! Shut up!" cried the gnome. He threw his hands up in the air and danced a jig as he shouted it over and over. "Shut up! Shut up! Shut up!"

Edna, Gemini and Puddlebrain stared at him with disgust. He'd helped them so they felt they owed him something, but now he was reverting to type – a nasty little gnome. It was no wonder he'd been thrown out of Templemead. If they had dared venture back upstairs, they'd gladly throw him out of their house. Without thinking, each of the sisters raised their hands at the same time and pointed at the current object of their displeasure.

"Shut UP!" they shouted, hurling a bolt of magic at, where a second before had danced the gnome.

The bolts, crackling whips of white light, smashed into each other in the centre of the triangle and splayed back out, hitting each of the witches simultaneously. They were thrown backwards, the wind knocked out of them, and lay gasping on the cellar floor.

"It's about time!" Billy said with a smile.

Chapter Thirteen

Under Puddlebrain's bed, where discarded items of clothing and half eaten sandwiches were normally kicked, the patch of darkness had spread. It oozed like oil across the floor, unfolding as if alive, making the floor and walls it touched almost seem to wilt. It was more focused now, less a vague blur as when it first appeared. It kept just within the confines of a normal shadow, barely able to contain itself, eager to stretch out as if it was just waking up.

Suddenly, it recoiled as if stung. It paused, sensing, waiting, *tasting*, then it shrank back slowly, becoming a concentrated blot of nothing. The colours of the carpet and wallpaper were left bleached and anaemic as if they had died without ever having lived and were now pallid ghosts of their former selves.

On the outskirts of town, in the break between Hill and Wood, the grass around the Hole leaned inwards, as if the Hole was sucking the air in. The intake was brief and the grass quickly returned to its former pride as a pale green cloud, dense to the point of being almost solid, rose up out of the pit and dissipated off towards the village.

Lem Artthorpe, born with a slab of dried lard where his consideration should have been, was sneaking back to the Town Square. He was one of a group of five villagers, all of whom were eager for vengeance but none of whom really knew why. Petral Gringe, Lemon's on-but-mainly-off girlfriend was beside him. There was a wildness to her eyes as if she didn't care what they were doing as long as it was done. To be honest, Petral often had a wild look in her eyes, but this was different. This wasn't the expression of mild insanity that Lem had grown to love (if he was honest with himself, which very rarely happened). It was the look of one who couldn't have stopped themselves from jumping off a cliff even if they'd had a vision of their mangled body at the base before they'd taken the leap.

Lem looked around him. His companions, Grail Benniton, Berry Briant and Henry What's-His-Face (what *was* his second name?) all had the same rampage-a-go-go air about them. For all Lem knew, the same look was in his eyes.

Oh well.

The witches would pay for what they'd most probably done to Quentin, especially now they'd potentially turned their possible powers onto dear old Brenda Corrigan. Who'd give him leftover jam tarts now, eh? Answer me that! So what if this was all based on a supposition that was part of a conjecture mingled in with an assumption with a little guessing thrown in for good measure? It was a real witches' brew, and *that* was the point.

It was actually the only point. Lem realised suddenly that they had picked on the witches purely because nobody *knew*. The witches, whom Lem actually quite liked, were the most obvious suspects when someone disappeared in the middle of the day, just like that, without a by-your-leave or a 'Catch you on the flap, Jack!' Ignoring the fact that they weren't precisely suspects, more scapegoats than anything, it *had* to be magic, so it *had* to be them. Even though it was widely known that they had lost their powers decades ago. And most people thought they were pretty OK. And most people never got themselves worked up about anything more important than running out of toilet paper at *just* the wrong moment…

They had reached the corner of the Town Square and Merrybone Way, the crescent shaped street they'd fled to after

Brenda had vanished. It was quite inconsiderate of her to do that, thought Lem. She spoiled a good burning, and there hadn't been one for centuries. Now they'd probably never get another chance – the moment had gone. They could have toasted teacakes, marshmallows and everything.

The group crouched against the front wall of the old Perryman place. It was unoccupied now – had been for a few years since old Perryman had passed away in his sleep. No one fancied undertaking the extensive renovations that needed to be done to make the house half so that it was left to fade away on its own. There was no front garden as the house opened right onto the pavement. Buster Perryman had been less of a gardener than he was a handyman, so anything more than the odd potted plant on his windowsill was a waste of time.

Lem, Petral, Grail, Berry and Henry leaned close against the wall under the window with Lem in front. He waited. Each of them held their breath while they listened for any indication the witches might be wreaking their collective vengeance. There was no sound other than the whisper of a breeze titillating the leaves of the trees that lined the street. Lem took the immense risk to his personal safety of peeking around the corner. He eased his head out, ready to snatch it back at any second. He daren't breathe in case the witches could hear him from the stake. He daren't think in case they could read his thoughts, terrified though those thoughts might be, and discover his hiding place as easily as if he'd jumped out waving his arms, shouting "Over 'ere!"

The stake was empty. The witches were gone. Lemon could see the cut ropes draped across the wooden pieces around the base. It was fine wood, that. Good kindling wood. Flare up in a heartbeat, that wood would.

The witches were gone. Lem gasped and turned back to his companions.

They were gone too. Only Petral's false top palate, the front teeth that she'd had replaced after falling from a horse she'd been trying to steal before remembering she couldn't ride, lay on the path. Lem picked them up. They were still wet. He carefully brushed a few pieces of grit from the dentures, spat on them, and slipped them into his own mouth. He'd been with Petral when she'd tried to steal that horse. He couldn't ride either. The teeth were a little uncomfortable, but they'd do.

It suddenly dawned on Lemon Artthorpe that perhaps Petral and the others hadn't simply gotten scared and fled. It also dawned on him, like the sun rising gloriously in that empty nighttime between his ears, that Petral wouldn't leave her top palate behind.

Ah.

Lem took a deep breath, and then promptly fainted.

Chapter Fourteen

The shadow beneath Puddlebrain's bed had recovered from whatever had ailed it - had made it recoil - and was spreading out once more. In a matter of scant seconds it had covered the whole floor of the bedroom, undulating like a lake of night, a ripple of nothing. It went still for a moment, then pulled itself inwards, the centre rising up as if pushed from beneath, the edges blurring back like steam on a windowpane. It rose to a height just short of six feet, then…

…It took form.

Human form.

Almost.

Where had once been nothing but a simple bed, a dumpy lamp with a shade that sat permanently cocked to one side in a 'Hey, I give the light around here. Me, you hear?' way perched haughtily atop a small table and a wardrobe that had never seemed to have seen better days, was now nothing *and* those items. A nothing that had shape. A nothing that had sense. A Nothing that had *something.*

A nothing that could move.

It was black, a soulless black that drained your heart if you stared at it for too long. It looked like a person that someone had forgotten to paint in – there were the shapes of arms and legs and what was obviously a head, but there were no features. It walked, actually *walked*, towards the bedroom door. It paused and the head moved as if it was looking at the wood, wondering what it was. A hand, with fingers of dusk, was raised towards the handle. It stopped. A ripple washed over the shape. It was laughing. With a sound like a wheel rolling through snow that had been in the sun too long and had almost turned to slush, the Nothing passed through the door.

In the cellar, Puddlebrain scratched her ear.

Chapter Fifteen

"Got an itch?" asked Gemini.

"Got fleas, more like," said Edna.

The sisters had managed to sit themselves up and brush themselves off. Dust mites still danced in the air, playing catch me if you can with the witches nostrils. Their faces were red and puffy and they were shaking. Billy stood to one side where he'd jumped to just before the witches had shot their magic at him. He had one hand on his hip and a foot resting on Edna's overturned stool.

"Don't you lot ever stop bickering?" he said. "It's *my* job to cuss and crow at you. You've been doing it yourself for years and look where it's got you - sitting on a dingy cellar floor with faces like pomegranates. Not exactly something to be proud of."

The sisters stared sullenly at that dingy cellar floor, apparently examining something that wasn't there but they wished was. Puddlebrain drew abstract pictures in the dust with her finger.

"I thought so," Billy said. "Nothing to say for yourself. Typical. Ninnies. That's what you are. Ninnies with a capital Nin." He stepped over Gemini's splayed legs and stood back in the middle of the room. "I can't believe such all powerful witches couldn't figure out such a simple thing."

"Oh…" Edna was going to say 'shut up' but thought better of it. She looked at the rosy faces of her sisters. Something had happened here, and she wasn't sure what.

"Shut up." It was the most intelligent thing she could think of to say in the end. She said it without much force, making the words feel like a deflated balloon breaking wind on the floor.

"How did you do that?" asked Gemini, as deflated as Edna's balloon.

"I didn't do anything," said the gnome. He spoke as if he were talking to a child, one who couldn't see the nose on their face or the spots in front of their eyes.

"But one minute you were there, and the next you'd gone! How did we miss you?"

Billy scratched his head. *He* wasn't the only thing they were missing. He knew Gemini was a meat pie short of a baker's dozen, but the other two were usually sharper than this.

"Oh, that," he said. "Just a little trick I learned back home. Comes in useful not to be in a certain place sometimes, especially when that certain place might get you hurt like, say, from a blast of *magic*."

"But how did you do it?" Gemini wanted to know.

He sat down facing Gemini. Puddlebrain and Edna were on either side still staring at the floor. Billy smiled gently, something that looked out of place on his gnarled old face. He took Gemini's hand in his and rubbed it softly.

"Tell me something," he said as gently as he was stroking her hand. "Do you suffer from neck or back ache?"

Gemini frowned. *What?*

"What?" she asked.

"Because you people are the *DENSEST* witches I've ever known!" Billy cried, flinging Gemini's hand down. He jumped to his feet. "It's a wonder you've lived as long as you have without magicking yourselves into oblivion the way you carry on!"

He circled the floor, shoving his face so close to theirs they could see the veins pulsing angrily in his forehead.

"Honestly! It takes you nearly eighty years to figure out the simplest thing and when you finally do, thanks to *me* I might add, you still don't see it! Open your eyes," he ranted. "Open your bimbling eyes!"

The witches stared at the gnome with blank expressions on their faces. What was he on about? How did he vanish when they shot their…

Ah.

Magic.

They shot their magic at him.

Ah.

The witches blinked. Their faces lit up as if the sun had suddenly risen in the combined twilight of their minds.

Ah indeed.

Billy saw the look on their faces as the witches' eyes met his. *Finally!* Oh, but he had his work cut out for him here!

"Well goody for you! It's finally sunk in! About time is all I can say!"

"You dived didn't you," said Gemini, looking so proud of herself she could burst like a ripe melon with her pinky finger. "You saw our hands come up and dived out of the way, that was all, wasn't it?"

Billy slapped his forehead in despair. So the ship had finally sunk in the harbour of Gemini's head. He just didn't believe this.

"Gemini" Edna snapped. "Think about it."

Puddlebrain nodded her head vigorously. "Yes. We've got it back. *We've got it back!*"

She jumped to her feet, forgetting the low ceiling. The ceiling, as ceilings often do, reminded her of its presence by not moving out of the way when her head collided with it. She sat back down with a thump, smiling insanely.

"We've got it back," she moaned. A bruise quickly decorated the top of her head, right at the hairline. It looked like a purple star commending her wondrous revelation.

"Yes, " Billy said. "That you did."

Gemini looked confused. "I wasn't aware we'd lost anything," she said. "I mean, I've misplaced my swan brooch that I like to wear on Sunday and Wednesday afternoons, but I'm sure it'll turn up sooner or later. I just have to stop looking for it then I'll find it. Things like that are always in the last place you look. I tried to make it the first place I looked but it didn't work. I guess that was because it wasn't the last…"

"Gemini!" Edna interrupted Your brooch is in the bottom of your wardrobe where it fell off your dress. That's where it always is! That's not what Puddlebrain means! We got *It* back!"

"It? It? What is *it*?" Her stomach groaned. She patted it understandingly. "Can we get something to eat? It must be well past thirteen o'clock by now."

Puddlebrain and Edna looked at each other and shook their heads. Their sister could be such a chore sometimes, and much worse than having to wash, dry and put away the dishes.

"Why don't you show her," suggested Billy.

Edna frowned. She wasn't sure just what magic had been recovered, let alone how it had happened. She might try to cast a spell and have it rebound on her simply because she was out of practice. That was certainly something she didn't want to risk – not again. But her sister was so slow sometimes, growing hair was faster. But what to try? How to show her?

Gemini's stomach growled again and Edna knew what to do. She lifted her hand hesitantly. She looked at Puddlebrain, who nodded briefly, obviously pleased it was Edna who was taking the risk. Even the gnome took a step backwards. It was a simple spell, one of the easiest to perform. The minimum flick was required, and that was all Edna gave it.

On the dusty cellar floor beside Gemini appeared a bowl. In the bowl, gurgling away happily, swam bladderwrack leaves in a thick chicken broth. Gemini's favourite. She made a grab for it and was just about to tip it to her mouth when she stopped suddenly, frozen as if she'd been stuck in a heartbeat and needed a kick to get started again. She put the bowl back down slowly, realization spreading across her face like a sunrise across a spring meadow, or in Gemini's case a well ploughed field.

"We got it back?" she whispered, flexing her fingers.

Chapter Sixteen

"I'm sure there's an echo in here somewhere," said Billy impatiently. "And it's about dingle-dangle time too!"

"How?" asked Edna.

Normally she'd be well on her way to shaking an explanation out of Billy by now, but she was too dazed from the enormity of what was happening to even think about it.

"How? It's so simple, I just don't see how you missed it. How did you lose your magic in the first place?"

There was a guilty silence from Edna, so Puddlebrain raised her hand slowly, as if she were still at school and wanted to go to the toilet.

"Yes?" prompted Billy.

Puddlebrain looked nervously at her older sister.

"Edna had an… erm… accident while she was arguing with that Mayor Harper person."

"Edna had an accident. That's right, if a little short of the real truth. Edna – Mayor – finger – silverfish, am I correct? I mean, I'm only a lonely gnome who you dragged into your lives to give them more… life! You haven't told me any of this, but from the odds and sods you've mentioned, that's about the size of it isn't it? Edna – Mayor – finger – silverfish. Oh, and frog."

"That's about it," said Puddlebrain meekly. She avoided Edna's glaring stare. Why should she feel guilty when it was, really, Edna's fault anyway?

"Right," said Billy. "And you can get that look off your face Miss SnootyBritches."

Edna gasped. How dare he! Billy took no notice.

"Sneers and snorts are all well and good, but they don't change the fact that your young sister there is actually correct. *You* had an accident, and you've spent the last seven decades getting over it. That's quite funny when you think that it would have only taken a couple of weeks, and that's only because you were still catching flies for a fortnight afterwards!"

Edna spluttered in response. Her face was going the colour of pomegranates. Her eyes were beginning to bulge.

"I…! I…! You…!" was all she could manage.

"Be still, Edna," hissed Puddlebrain. "Billy's right. I don't know how, but he is. Calm down and just listen instead of ploughing in."

Being attacked from two sides at once, and one of those being her sister, was too much for the older witch. She crossed her arms and sullenly fumed on her own. Gemini wasn't used to the mighty Edna being treated like this and couldn't help but smirk. A glare from the other quickly made her realise that perhaps it wasn't as funny as she thought, though she'd possibly disagree – to herself, in her mind, at night in the dark.

Puddlebrain nodded to the gnome to carry on. Billy was glad that there was at least one semi-rational person in the room, apart from himself that was.

"What happened?" she asked.

"Don't you know? Isn't it obvious?" Billy looked at the blank faces of the witches. They didn't know, and it was obviously as obvious as how it could be thirteen o'clock three times a day for Gemini when a clock only went up to twelve. Billy sighed. "It took anger and thoughtlessness to block your magic, not take it away as you thought, so it took anger and thoughtlessness to unblock it! Qualities you three have in ample measure."

"And that was it?" Puddlebrain asked.

"That was it. Even I, a lowly gnome, could figure that one out. You were just trying too hard. All your chanting and huddling around the big soup dish over the years was a complete waste of time." He smiled. "Quite funny when you think about it, don't you think?"

"FUNNY!" cried Edna.

Her face was crimson now. If she'd been a kettle she would have been boiling, splashing scalding water hither and thither.

"*Funny*, is it?"

Her arms were waving in the air. Billy ducked to make sure he wasn't hit by a stray bolt of magic – that was, after all, how the witches 'lost' their powers in the first place.

"Edna!" snapped Puddlebrain. "Be quiet! Billy was *helping* us, yet again. Remember he just saved our lives? Leave him be and stop being so pompous!"

Edna stared at her sister and Gemini curled up into a ball and started giggling. Billy was impressed. He'd never heard either of the younger witches stand up to Edna. It was quite refreshing.

"Look," he said finally. "You just had to… recreate what happened back then, more or less. It took three simultaneous hits to lose your magic, and it needed three to get it back again. You had to *not* think about it and just *do*. Anyway, if all I'm going to get is mouth and hassle, I'll leave you to your happy little band of marauders and be on my way!"

He turned and made to go to the door but Edna grabbed his leg. She looked sheepish, which, as it wasn't an expression she wore that often, didn't suit her. She much preferred being the wolf.

"Sorry," she croaked. It was the best she could manage.

"Haven't you three enjoyed having no magic to help you?" Billy asked.

Gemini had recovered from her giggles and had become more focused, a feat and a half for the witch.

"Enjoyed not having magic?" she said. "Are you mad?"

"Well, your house pretty much looks after itself, and you, but what about cooking meals and sweeping up and walking and all that normal stuff. Hasn't it been fun, or at least a worthwhile experience?"

All three witches frowned. Why would walking be fun? What was worthwhile about having to wait hours for a simple broth to be bubbling happily away? The gnome had obviously been nice for too long and it was having an adverse effect on him. He was going crazy.

"No," said Gemini simply. "It was not fun."

"Oh well," sighed Billy. "It was just a thought. I wondered if you might have learned anything from your experience."

"Only to aim better next time!" said Edna.

"And to duck quicker," mumbled Puddlebrain.

"Anyway," said Edna, reverting back to her normal I'm-in-charge attitude. "Thanks."

Billy smiled, then remembered himself. He'd become a little lost in the moment and had softened. Can't be having that! "Whoa!" he exclaimed. "Just watch yourself there witch! Don't think you can be nice to me all of a sudden!"

"As if I would," Edna smiled. "Not a chance."

Puddlebrain smiled too. They had their powers again. It meant they could face the villagers if they came back.

The villagers…

"Erm…" she began.

Chapter Seventeen

Brimley Baltimore was the richest man in Little Whimsy. By comparison to the rest of the town, he was wealthy beyond their dreams. He had money coming out of his ears, some claimed. If he coughed, he'd choke on a coin. If he farted, it smelled of gold. Now Brimley didn't know exactly what gold smelled of, as he'd never actually had any close enough to his nose to get a whiff, but he did admit to being quite well off. Being wealthy beyond the dreams of the Whimsy folk didn't really amount to much as their inbred lethargy meant they didn't usually have much to dream about, but that was ok. Brimley more than made up for them.

The Baltimore residence, as Brimley called his house, was spacious and proud. It lay just down the street from the Manor House, home to the current Mayor of Little Whimsy. The two houses were similar in size, but the Baltimore residence (*house* was far too common a term for such a grand monument to architectural engineering – or some such nonsense) was by far the most impressive. The Manor House had been left to the pleasures of the wind and the rain over the years, mainly due to it remaining empty for around twelve or so years until the mayor decided it was more suited to his haughty position than the little two-up, three-down he'd lived in previously.

In Brimley's case, he'd started with his own simple two-up, three-down that was dwarfed by the Manor, and extended and built and designed and patched until it was a real home to be reckoned with – a habitat with attitude. Seven bedrooms were more than ample for Brimley and his fairly small family, but so what? Four living rooms, three dining rooms and a pantry in a plum tree, the size of Windermere's back garden, might be a little excessive, but what did it matter? If you've got it, flaunt it, that was Brimley Baltimore's philosophy and he lived it to the full.

A glorious fountain in the shape of a hawk diving for a doomed rodent, the water spraying from the back-swept wings to give the illusion of great speed, occupied the front garden. It was ornately surrounded by various brightly coloured plants that blazed in the sunlight, the names of which Brimley couldn't remember and never intended to find out. All the windows of the house were frosted with images of animals and birds many of which no one this side of the Aren Rush's sister river, the Swell, had even heard of. The inspiration for the images came from the journals of Hector Ramsdale, the renowned explorer and shoemaker who had travelled from one end of the world to the other and back again, just to try out the luxuriously comfortable new shoes he'd created.

Doors two men high and at least four wide provided entry into the lavish hall which was dominated by a winding staircase leading into the extensive depths of the upper floor. Every room was of equal splendour - a palace that was as out of place in Little Whimsy as Gemini would be in the top form of Quentin Bopsidy's school.

Brimley wasn't a king, nor was he an earl or even a mayor. He was simply an ordinary Joe who'd chanced upon a little luck. He'd tell you it hadn't changed him. He'd say he was the same man who used to sing in the Town Square for loose change on a Sunday afternoon. He'd assure you he would, if he ever had the time, continue to entertain the children with his puppet shows after school on Wednesdays, just as he did when he was an ordinary Joe, which, of course, he still was. He wasn't conceited, Mr. Brimley Baltimore, he was merely a little misguided. Perhaps, though he'd be loath to admit it, his 'little luck' *had* gone to his head, just a teensy bit.

Opposite the doorway to the third living room (or the second if you were counting from the other way) was a small, non-descript door. It was the sort of thing you'd walk past without seeing, like a painting that had hung on the wall above the fire for so long, it was part of the background. A memory that you never remembered. It had a round handle, tarnished brass that had the grime and sweat of years worn into it. The door and its handle were about the only remnants of the house that had existed pre-little-luck. A stairway led down on the other side. It spiralled vertically in a tight coil into the darkness below.

On the wall at the foot of the staircase was a hook for a lamp which, when lit, flickered as if the flames were moths trying to escape the confines of the glass. A corridor, low and tight like the stairs, led a short way to a small bare room. A table was the only occupant of the room, and that was there purely to stand the lamp on while busying oneself with the real reason for the 'invisible' door, the tightly wound stairs and the cramped corridor.

Across from the entrance to the room, was a large, heavy steel door hung on massive hinges. It was triple locked with a combination of combination locks and a great stonking padlock that took all Brimley's strength to lift it. Behind this behemoth of a door was a vault. Within the vault, resting leisurely on a cushion that in turn rested upon a stone pedestal, was the source of Brimley Baltimore's fortune.

The door was hanging open. No matter how the hinges were oiled or greased, they always creaked, a sharp, vicious sound in the closeness of the vault and the room. Brimley was standing in front of the pedestal, staring at his treasure, lost in thought. Nowadays, when he wasn't out thinking of different ways to spend, this was where he'd be. Looking without seeing, present in body, but with his mind having wandered off back to when he found it. It was his favourite time – that few moments out of his entire life when he had something new and exciting and magical in his hands. Granted, he still had possession of his prize, but back when he originally found it, well *that* was special.

'It' was a small black leather purse. 'It' had a worn drawstring that threatened to snap whenever it was pulled. 'It' was basically a bag with a gather at the top and a cord to pull it shut. 'It' was nothing less than that, but it was also so much more.

Brimley had been walking back from the school. It was a Wednesday evening and he had not long finished another successful puppet show. He had introduced a pair of new characters, a cat and its owner, a wizened old woman who couldn't hear very well and kept sneezing – though she insisted she wasn't allergic to cats, and the children had loved them. He was smiling and looking forward to the sausage casserole that would be waiting for him when he arrived home.

It was hot. The sun was a blazing blur in the clear sky and Brimley had taken his ash-hair coat off to cool down. Ash hair was all very well on cooler days, and wasn't so bad on the run up to winter when the temperature could drop like a stone in the river, then splash back up to fool you into thinking it was still the leftovers of summer. For a hot day, however, the fur of the ash was simply too much. Besides, when it got hot, it itched. He was pleased he'd left his puppets at the school for the children to play with, rather than lug the heavy case home in this heat. It was evening. It was meant to be cooler in the evenings, but right now could easily have been noon.

He was nearing his street, from the opposite end to the grand Manor House, and had paused to pick a few wild flowers for Mary, his wife.

"Romance is my middle name," he'd tell her after springing a surprise present or box of chocolates on her.

"Funny," she'd say. "I thought it was Edward."

They'd laugh at their jokes and life would be good and life would be happy.

Brimley didn't see it at first. His hands were almost full with Lilies, Queen Anne's Lace and Black Eyed Susan brimming over his fingers. He plucked a rose as if it were a grey hair from his head – a sharp tug and it was in his hand. The purse was out of sight. It was away beneath a bush that was more thorn than leaf, almost as if it were hiding, or perhaps hidden. Perhaps it had been secreted by an unknown owner.

He thought it was a lump of mud, or a stone lazily sleeping in the summer heat. It wasn't until he was about to stand that he saw that it was neither. He reached in slowly, careful of the barbs on the bush, and pulled it out. It was light, obviously not full. Brimley looked around to see if anyone was nearby that might have dropped the purse. The street was empty. It did, to his credit, occur to him that maybe he should just put it back and walk away. There didn't seem to be much inside, but times were tough and even a few coppers helped keep the wolves from the door and the rain from coming through the roof.

His indecision lasted a few seconds, and then Brimley Baltimore did the one thing that changed his life forever. He stuck his fingers into the closed top of the purse and spread them. The purse opened like a flower in the morning sun, its leaves spreading to let in the hungry bees. He peeked inside. There were a few coins. Not gold – that was too much to expect, but it certainly looked like there wes a piece of silver or two. He tipped them into his palm and nodded to himself. Not bad, he thought. Enough to treat his wife to dinner at Corrigan's, perhaps. He scooped up the flowers from where he'd dropped them to examine the purse then turned and started towards his house, absent-mindedly tossing the purse back into the undergrowth.

Then he stopped. He turned back and looked down to where the purse had landed. It was almost exactly where he had picked it up from, concealed beneath the thorn bush. That wasn't, though, what had stooped Brimley Baltimore in his tracks.

The empty purse had jingled as it landed.

Brimley paused. Brimley frowned. Then, Brimley stooped and picked up the empty purse that was, strangely, no longer empty. It was still open – after all, why close an empty one? It wasn't as if the air was going to fall out. He pocketed the coins he already had and emptied the purse into his palm once more. Again it was a mixture of silver and coppers. Not a great deal, but more than nothing. Brimley bit his lip as he held the leather bag upright again. He shook it. It jingled. Again, he poured its contents into his hand and again it was the same.

Brimley took a deep breath. He was scared, elated and jittery as a jug-a-bug all at the same time. He put the coins in his pocket. His heart was beating faster than a startled horse. Beads of sweat popped out for a run down his forehead. His hands shook slightly. He repeated the sequence – tilt bag up, tilt it down, pour it out – three more times until he thought his trousers would be down to his ankles from the weight in his pockets.

He could scarcely breathe and his throat was dry. He licked his lips and swallowed, making a hard sound like an egg plopping through a small hole. Looking around nervously, he saw he was the only person in sight. Running as fast as he could without the change in his pockets bouncing away along the road or his pants falling down and tripping him up, he hurried home, the magical purse gripped in his hands as if it were the last loaf of bread in a starving world – except Brimley Baltimore didn't think he'd ever starve again.

Chapter Eighteen

That was a long time ago. Brimley had seemed to the people of Little Whimsy to have suddenly prospered, something he put down to an old rich uncle from Upper Bibsbury dying and leaving him his estate. Upper Bibsbury was just too far away for anyone to bother investigating, and was renowned for being a town where you couldn't get in if you didn't have quite a good few numbers on your bank balance. As such, Brimley's story was more or less accepted, and most thought good luck to the bloke. He was a decent sort. Money wouldn't change him, and if it did, he'd brought plenty of smiles to the youngsters, so they guessed it was ok.

For a long time, it didn't change Brimley. But money has its own methods and madness, and before too long Brimley had succumbed. He grew distant from his wife, and forgot his Wednesday evening shows. His house grew, but his life, such as it was, shrank in direct proportion. He became, not obsessed, but enthralled by his treasure. He had to check it was still there, hidden away in his vault, on a daily, then hourly, then almost constant basis. He had been a tubby man, well rounded and jolly. He became thin and gaunt. A constant shadow shaded his eyes, as his mind was never far from his prize. His fingers twitched to be holding the purse. In the end, his whole body twitched if he wasn't in its presence.

Brimley didn't talk to it, but he was sure, sometimes, late at night when he lay awake in his bed and long after his wife was asleep, that he could hear *it* whispering to *him.* That was at night though, when you could even have conversations with the wind if you felt inclined, or you might want to draw the curtains if the moon was too bright and you were sure it was watching you.

During the day, Brimley was much more lucid. Lucid, yet still under the spell of the bottomless purse. This spell was what found him, as ever, standing before the pedestal, lost in his memories. Somewhere in his mind, tucked neatly away right at the back, it was possible that he missed his old life. It was a simpler time then and he used to smile a lot. But those thoughts, if they existed, were buried, swept away by greed and craving. Without thinking his hand reached out to the purse. He just wanted a few coins to line his pockets. He felt more comfortable that way. It helped him get through the day.

His fingers were inches from the purse. Then, they weren't. The vault door hung open on its great hinges. The moth-like flame still skittered in the lamp. The corridor was dark. The stairs were tight. The purse, font of an endless supply of money, lay peacefully on its cushion atop the stone pedestal.

Otherwise the room was empty.

At the far end of Shadowmoss Lane, at the top of the stairs that led from the witches' bedrooms, the walking shadow paused and rippled. It seemed suddenly larger. More imposing. It moved to the first step and started down to the ground floor.

Chapter Nineteen

In the dusty, dingy cellar, Puddlebrain scratched her ear.

"Nits?" asked Edna.

Puddlebrain glared at her sister. "A fly or something, actually."

Edna raised her eyebrows questioningly. Hmmm. Not convinced. Something bothered her and she couldn't quite remember what it was.

"Anyway," continued Puddlebrain. "We've got more important things to think about. We've just been spared a good roasting for one thing. Brenda Corrigan might well have followed Quentin, but I'm pretty sure the rest haven't and they'll be baying for our blood before too long."

Billy nodded his head. "The lady speaks sense. Amazing."

Puddlebrain ignored the gnome's comment and carried on.

"We have to either get out of here or find out what really happened."

Gemini shook her head vehemently. "Why should we care about that lot?" she wanted to know. "After what they just did? Let them disappear themselves off if they feel like it! Good riddance to bad rubbish, that's what I say"

Edna leaned forward. "I agree, Gemini. But if it's the only way to prove we didn't do it, we might have no choice." She leaned back again, confidently. "Besides, we've got our magic back now. If they don't believe us in the end, we'll disappear them off after their friends ourselves."

Billy frowned. "And back to your natural form you slip," he sneered. "That sort of talk is how you got into a mess in the first place. You need to…"

Billy stopped. The furrow on his forehead deepened. He was staring at the locked and bolted doorway.

A black shape, man-size and menacing, had just melted through the door.

"What…?"

The witches looked at him. Edna opened her mouth to speak, but the shadow touched her on the back of the head and she vanished. The thing rippled. Gemini went to scream, her eyes wide, but she didn't get the chance. Moving like water across glass, the black mass slid over and touched her too. She disappeared.

There was no sound. There was no flash. They were there, and then they were not.

Billy scrambled backwards as it moved towards him, but it ignored the gnome and headed for the remaining witch.

Puddlebrain knew she didn't have anywhere to run to. The cellar was too low and cramped to do anything, not that she would have known what to do anyway.

A glob of night stretched out from the shadow and reached for her. Instinctively she raised her arm, her finger pointing.

There was a flash and a shriek and the thing was gone, hit by a shot from Puddlebrain's hand.

The shriek faded slowly, almost dripping from the witch's ears. Billy crawled forward, for the first time having nothing to say. Puddlebrain lowered her arm carefully. Her ears were ringing from the sound the thing had made before it disappeared –like a thousand people all screaming at once. She looked around her. Apart from herself, the gnome and a few hundred dizzy specks of dust, the cellar was empty.

"W…?"

"Indeed," answered Billy. "I think we've just seen what happened to Mr. Bopsidy."

Puddlebrain shook her head to try and rattle some sanity back in. It didn't seem to work. Her sisters really had departed. She really had blasted a walking shadow into nothing – although how nothing could be blasted into nothing... It dawned on the witch that she may well have just destroyed the only thing that might have been able to bring her sisters back. Puddlebrain began to cry.

Seventy years of frustration at being a half-witch (or in Gemini's case a half-wit-witch) piled onto being kidnapped, smothered with barely escaping being main course at the town barbeque, topped neatly with losing her sisters was just too much for her. She wept, her hands over her face and her shoulders shuddering with each sob. Her cries and moans filled the cellar, making its enclosed spaces seem even more suffocating. Billy felt as if he were being crushed. He had an idea of what the witch must be feeling, but this wasn't the time, and certainly not the place, to fall apart over it. He slapped her. Puddlebrain instantly stopped crying and dropped her hands, stunned.

Hmmm, thought Billy. *That felt quite refreshing!*

He raised his hand to have another go, but a warning stare from Puddlebrain stopped him. The look told him that if he tried it, he might well be following the shadow thing on the next wagon into oblivion. Well, at least she'd sort of calmed down, even if she was still blubbering a bit. It was better than nothing. The gnome wasn't insensitive to her problems, not at all. But he was a gnome. These lapses of concern and friendliness were obviously some disease he'd picked up while being in Little Whimsy. He just couldn't help himself. But the gnome in him helped keep them in check and keep the problems at hand in focus.

"Look Puddlebrain," he said, putting on his best *I'm-here-for-you* voice and trying to keep the hint of *if-I-must-be* out of it. "Snivelling won't bring your sisters back from wherever they've decided to hop off to. It also won't stop the entire village, or what might be left of it, from banging your doors down and having you for breakfast. We need to do something."

"But they're *gone!*" Puddlebrain whined.

"Yes. They are. Full marks for spotting that one. Go to the top of the class."

Puddlebrain gave him a look that would wither a sapling at twenty paces. He ignored it.

"But what you don't seem to see," he continued, "is that, when Brenda Corrigan vamoosed, there was no black whatever-it-was hanging around joining in the party!"

Puddlebrain thought about it. Billy was right. Brenda had simply disappeared. Gone in a flash – except without the flash. But so what?

"And?" she asked. She had stopped crying now, and her sniffs were subsiding. She wiped her nose on her sleeve without thinking about it. For the first time in centuries she really did feel like the baby of the family, even though she was a good three times as old as anyone else in the village and she didn't, right at this moment, actually have any family.

Billy crouched down. She had shown so much promise only moments before. "I don't think that thing was really what has been taking everyone. I think it was just… an agent or something."

"An agent? For whom? And why?"

"Well, come on. I'm good, but I'm not that good! I don't know. Something or someone else. Something is taking the residents of Little Whimsy for whatever purpose. And it took your sisters too."

Puddlebrain sat up straight. Her mind was moving slowly from the negative to the positive. She was no longer thinking about losing her sisters, but of finding them again. If she had to find the others at the same time, well, you couldn't have everything. She'd make allowances.

"Well, that's fine for Brenda and probably Quentin, but why did that thing come for my sisters? And why didn't it take me?"

"I don't think you gave it a chance, little Miss FireFinger. You want to be careful where you wave that thing around. Anyway, maybe your magic made it more difficult to just take you, and something more was needed. Maybe it needed some sort of personal touch?"

Puddlebrain nodded her head, not that anything really made any sense. The shadow *had* made physical contact with Edna and Gemini. Perhaps being a witch gave them some sort of protection or additional barrier. They couldn't just be whisked off. The extra defence hadn't particularly helped her sisters, but it could have made it harder. This was all guesswork, but that was all they had.

"Could be," she said. "But what now? Where do we start? How do we get out of here to begin with?"

"Getting out of here is the least of our worries," Billy said. "The villagers, if there are any left, all think you're responsible. Just show them your finger and they'll probably run a mile. As for where… I don't know. This is your village. You tell me."

"I don't know. It could be anywhere!"

Billy tapped the side of his nose thoughtfully. It sprung from side to side in a hypnotic rhythm that held her gaze and stilled her scattered thoughts.

"I doubt you'll find it in a sunny meadow or a playground," mused the gnome. "It'll be somewhere people veer away from. Where is the darkest, scariest place you know?"

Puddlebrain frowned. Dark and scary. Dark and scary. Dark and…

Chapter Twenty

"*Grimace Woods*!" she exclaimed. "It has to be. Nobody ever goes there. My father was the only person I know to have actually spent any length of time in the woods, and he never spoke of it."

Billy nodded.

"Well, it's a start," he said. "Let's go."

"Just like that? Now?"

Puddlebrain was scared already, before they'd even left the house. She wasn't used to doing this taking action sort of thing, especially without her sisters to back her up.

"We have to start somewhere and somewhen. So Grimace Woods and Now it is. Come on."

It was all very well making it to the woods, but...

"Then what?" she asked.

"Then we see!" Billy sighed. "How do I know? We might not find anything there. Or what we are looking for might very well be hiding in the woods, and find *us!* I don't know. Now come *on!*"

Puddlebrain knew it was no use fighting. She couldn't simply sit and wait it out. Well… She could… No. No she couldn't. She took a deep breath, which failed to calm her nerves, and stood up – as much as she could considering the low ceiling. Billy went to the door and threw back the bolts. He gingerly pulled it open and peered out. The stairway up to the hall was gloomy but there was enough light to see that no one was lying in wait. He moved onto the first step which, naturally, creaked. He held his breath, as if doing so might make the sound go unheard. There was no movement. All he could hear was his own heartbeat and Puddlebrain's nervous breaths. He gestured to the witch to follow. Together they crept up to the ground floor.

The house was silent. The lack of noise was all the more eerie due to the fact that the house was *never* this quiet. There was always a racket – arguing, chatting, slurping (at the many thirteen o'clocks) and, at night, snoring. It emphasised how alone Puddlebrain was and she almost began to cry again. Almost. If she wanted her sisters back, and today was probably the first time she'd ever admit to such a thing, it wouldn't happen if she fell to blubbering pieces at every turn.

She went into the living room to look outside. The heavy curtains were still closed so she didn't have to crawl, but she did so anyway. Carefully pulling them apart, Puddlebrain could see the whole length of Shadowmoss Lane. It was empty. Billy's voice next to her made her jump.

"What can you see?"

"Don't *do* that!" she hissed, almost having to catch her heart leaping out of her chest.

Billy, even under these circumstances, couldn't help but snigger.

"Sorry," he said, not entirely convincingly. "Is anyone out there?"

Puddlebrain took another look to make sure. There was no one about.

"Not a soul that I can see. Of course that doesn't mean they're not hiding."

"Well, we can't do anything about that. We've got to go sooner or later so I say sooner, because there might not be a later."

Puddlebrain nodded, resigned.

"I suppose we're just going to have to risk it."

"Hey, don't be so down. Remember you've got your magic back. That should do us some good, even if it's only to scare off any roaming villagers."

The witch, who was, actually, a real witch once more, managed a smile. She wasn't accustomed to the idea of having her powers returned yet. Seventy years was a long time and, even though they'd been trying to get them back and really wouldn't let on, they had become used to not being witches. Puddlebrain had to admit that to herself. They were still far from normal – their long lives were testament to that fact – but their witchiness was, sometimes, as if it had been part of someone else, someone that they used to know. To go back to being that someone else would take a little getting used to.

"Let's go," she said in a manner that showed she was ready.

Inside, she was far from ready. Inside, Puddlebrain wanted Edna to be here to tell her what to do. She wanted Gemini here to feel superior to (which wasn't a very nice attitude but one that was difficult not to have around her). Unfortunately, Edna wasn't here and there was a great big question mark hanging, like a hammer waiting to fall, over whether Edna would ever be here again. Gemini wasn't here either, and that same hammer was hanging over her – a practical toolbox of uncertainty.

Sigh.

Well, here goes.

Puddlebrain dropped the curtains and strode purposefully to the front door with Billy hurrying along behind. Without thinking, she waved her hand at the door, which gladly opened, pleased that the 'old' Puddlebrain was back, and walked out into the waiting world.

Chapter Twenty One

Nobody sprang on them as they stepped out. No rocks were thrown and no one started yelling at abuse. Shadowmoss Lane, from their position at the bottom right up to Windermere's house at the far end, was deserted. An eerie silence had descended, like a spider on a thread in the darkest night, that seemed somehow different to a normal quiet day. On a 'normal' day, like yesterday for example – though yesterday felt as if it was at least week and a half ago – you could still feel *life* in the air. Even if you couldn't actually hear anything, there was still a sense of activity, the knowledge that someone, somewhere, was doing *something*. Now there was nothing. Even Puddlebrain's breath seemed flat and listless, the substance dissolving as it exited her body.

"Hello?" Billy whispered.

He was feeling it too. He wasn't speaking to anyone in particular, but wanted to hear a voice, even if it was his own. He sounded as lifeless as the air, as if the energy was being sucked out of his words the second they left his mouth. Witch and gnome shuddered at the same time. Whose stupid idea was this?

"Come on," whispered Puddlebrain. Now they were out, they may as well get on with it.

The pair had left the house by the front door and now moved around to the back of the house. They went carefully, but with their pace matching their anxiety – they were not going to dawdle. It wasn't simply that they felt the need to hurry in their rescue attempt, but also that they didn't want to stay in one place for any length of time.

They felt as if they were being watched without anyone being near.

Turning right, they crossed over to Perryville Lane. Houses lined the road like soldiers standing to attention, preparing to attack the witch and gnome if they so much as dared to cross the threshold of the street. Having no other choice, they did just that. It occurred to Billy that they should, perhaps, move carefully, taking to the back gardens of the homes so as not to be seen.

"Listen," said Puddlebrain, her voice sounding almost comatose in the still air. "I don't think there's anyone left."

"I know what you mean," said Billy. "I don't think there's anyone left either, at least none of the villagers."

Puddlebrain looked at him, reading the intent in the gnome's words. No, Mrs. Mead wasn't baking any pies and no, Mrs. Burrows wasn't taking notice of everyone else's business except her own. Mr. Burrows wasn't asleep in his armchair either and nor was Ethel Ribblesbottom tending her cats. But that didn't mean the shadow that had taken her sisters wasn't coming after them or even if there were more of the creatures.

But what if there were?

It had found them hidden away in their cellar. Skipping from back garden to back garden wouldn't throw whatever it was off their scent and they ran the risk of running into rampaging villagers at every turn, so they couldn't hide from that either. The only real option, except to turn and run (but run where?), was to bite the banjo and walk right down the middle of the street. Beggar the lot of them. At least if they were in the open, they could see any trouble coming.

So, the middle of the street it was. Open and vulnerable and scared. They could feel eyes boring into them from every window, but knew the houses where empty. They expected to be charged at from every angle but no attackers appeared. A smothering sense of being alone only served to increase their wariness.

Small, unsteady steps. It was all they could manage at first. The boldness had washed out of both the witch and the normally brash gnome like dirt from a cloth, leaving them feeling limp and decidedly wet. Puddlebrain kept looking behind them to make sure they weren't being followed while Billy's head looked like it wasn't connected to his stumpy neck properly the way it was swivelling this way and that so much.

"This is ridiculous!" hissed Puddlebrain. "We'll never get anywhere at this rate. If we're running scared, how are we meant to stand up to whatever is going on?"

"Right you are," agreed Billy, "but you don't just pick up courage whilst walking down the street. It's not lying in stinky little piles, left by wandering horses who needed a little relief. And it doesn't drop on you from the sky like sparrow poop."

"Then let's pretend! Let's just pretend we're brave and just get on with it!"

Pretend? An interesting idea. Could they imagine they weren't scared and that would make them not be afraid? Could they wade on in with magic fingers a-blazing and fool the world into thinking they were alright with all of this? Billy doubted it. The problem was, up until now, he had been the strong-willed one. It had been he who had figured out the witches' problem. It had been he who had kicked some guts into Puddlebrain to get her started. Maybe he had gone too far. Perhaps he'd given her so much nerve, she had somehow soaked some of his up too, like an emotional sponge. Maybe, though, Billy simply wasn't as brave as he liked to think he was.

Nah. As if?

"Right," he said, holding his head up high (or as high as a gnome could anyway). "Away we go."

Puddlebrain smiled, although she had, deep down, hoped he might have suggested turning back. The pair walked purposefully along Perryville Lane. They stared straight ahead, partly to feign courage and partly because they knew if they kept looking around they might actually see something – something they really didn't want to see. The feeling of being under some malicious scrutiny stayed with them as they walked, but they did their best to ignore it. Why worry? If they were going to be taken, it was going to happen. Worrying about it didn't change the inevitable, it merely messed with your head until the inevitable arrived – inevitably.

Chapter Twenty Two

Within a few moments they had arrived at the Crossroads, crossing over it without pausing for breath. Fieldview Avenue, the straight, not a hiccup in sight, road that ended at the Field, stretched before them. Years ago, it had actually been an avenue, lined with fine elms that brightened the senses as you strolled beneath their branches.

The winter, seventeen years before, had put paid to that though.

Anything wooden became a victim of the fires that burned almost constantly to keep the bitter temperatures at bay. Beds were chopped up for fuel, as were gates and fences. Even Benny Greensome's wooden leg, a result of a drunken accident with a saw four years earlier, failed to escape. The elms burned well, and put up a good fight, but it was no good. The winter had lasted for four months, and it was the most blisteringly cold four months in living memory – and that included the witches' memory. It was seen that the sacrifices made by the likes of the elms and Benny were in a good cause. The fact that Benny had actually been accosted and robbed of his wooden leg rather than it being requested nicely, with a few coins and a dozen oven baked scones for the inconvenience, seemed to be conveniently forgotten.

Fieldview Avenue had a few houses close to the Crossroads end, but they petered out along its length, leaving only a few stragglers to remind anyone that this was a village and not just a track in the middle of nowhere. By the time three quarters of its extent had been passed, only overgrown grasses and weeds lined the road. If anything, this was more alarming than back when it had been houses on either side. Even a simple breeze manufactured movement in the grass causing Puddlebrain and Billy to catch their breath and quicken their step. By the time they reached the muddy track that marked Little Whimsy's boundary they were running – well, she was jogging and he, with his spindly little legs, was pretty much sprinting.

They stopped at the edge of the Field, panting The pair looked across the freshly cut grass (good old Nathan and his shears – it might take him a week at a time, but he was still the best gardener this side of anywhere) to where Grimace Woods, dark, foreboding and menacing to any who might be contemplating entry, loomed. Puddlebrain shivered. Billy would have done but he was too busy trying to breathe normally.

Oak. Almost every tree in Grimace Woods was oak. Other, lesser trees occasionally tried their luck and had a go at growing, but it was always in vain. The mighty and majestic oak was too proud to allow any interloper in their territory. Mighty and majestic.

Perhaps not quite the correct words to describe the abominations that dwelled within the Grimace.

It was rightly named. A more appropriate label hadn't been given since the Crossroads had been named as such. It wasn't that looking at the woods made you grimace, it was more that the trees were grimacing at *you*! The way their trunks twisted in a sneer. The way their branches clawed at the air in terrible anger. The darkness that settled in and between them like a slumbering pet, from which the light had fled in terrible fear. They were a grimace right enough and the air of dormant, yet still potent, threat that wrapped the Grimace in its blanket of menace did nothing to change that point of view.

But how? Why did they grow so? In other places, whether as a forest or as an individual, oaks were most definitely magnificent and proud and truly mighty. Why was the Grimace any different? Nobody knew. Nobody, not even the witches, had lived long enough to see the trunks twist or the branches claw. It had always been that way. It was best to just keep away. There were a few stories, naturally, of foolhardy folk who had succumbed to their foolhardy curiosity. Those who returned from the woods never spoke of what they saw and never slept a full night again. Those that didn't return… well, who knows? Usually, though, the look, the air, the feel was enough.

If you wanted to smile tomorrow, you'd never Grimace today.

It was one of those unspoken rules, like never standing in front of stampeding horses or never drinking milk that you could slice. You didn't need telling, at least not twice.

And it was into this nightmare that the witch and the gnome now headed. They didn't stop to think as they set off once more. Damp grass cuttings painted their shoes bright green as they walked across the field. Neither spoke. There was nothing to say apart from mentioning that this was a very bad idea – and neither wanted to hear the truth right at that moment.

The Field was basically an expanse of grass, mostly flat. A pair of old wooden benches sat side-by-side over towards the left. They were not near a path – there were no paths – and nor were they facing any particular direction. They were simply there, next to each other, keeping one another company.

A low fence, little more than a few planks nailed together, began a few yards up from the Little Whimsy sign. It ended only a few yards further on, an undertaking undertaken by a typically enthusiastic Whimsyan sometime ago. It had been intended that the fence would stretch right along the edge of the field, but whoever had started it had become bored. There hadn't even been enough wood to warrant theft during that particularly nasty winter. Apart from these features, such as they were, the only other element that wasn't small, green and wavy in the wind was the Hill.

Puddlebrain and Billy were nearing the Hill. It rose like a pimple on the face of the Field and seemed to draw them on, perhaps because it was the only real point of reference in the monotony. As they touched its leading edge, where the ground started to rise (or the pimple began to fester), they veered off slightly, heading towards a small clearing between two of the oaks that looked like a gap in the teeth of the Grimace. They didn't notice the Hole and didn't see the faintly greenish shimmer that hovered over its maw like a mouldy heat haze.

At the clearing, the pair stopped. Neither wanted to be the first to enter the Grimace. Billy would have liked to be the brazen gnome he'd always been. A few trees and a bit of darkness were nothing to be afraid of, were they? Looking into the woods, he couldn't see anything scary. Sure, some of the trees were bent at odd angles, but these were big trees. They would each have been fighting for their own patch of sunlight. They could quite easily end up misshapen and warped. As for the silence, all he could hear was his heart beating somewhere in his throat and the blood racing through his head as if it was trying to run away but had nowhere to go.

Puddlebrain, on the other hand, was happy being the quiet, usually unassuming witch she always was. She was afraid and didn't mind admitting it. Striding out of their house and marching all the way here was one thing. They could pretend to not be afraid. This was different. This was *Grimace Woods.* You could feel the nastiness clinging to your arms, plucking at the little hairs there. You could feel it running its greasy fingers through your hair.

the forest's web, a fly caught fast and waiting for whatever passed for a spider in the Grimace to come calling.

Then they were through. Both fell forward, released from whatever had held them. Billy was panting, his tunic stained with sweat. Puddlebrain stood trembling, one hand to her forehead and the other against the bark of an oak, then she fainted, collapsing in a heap across the gnarled roots. Billy rushed to her side.

He wasn't a doctor. He knew nothing about giving first, or even tenth aid. Gnomes, by their very nature, were not disposed to helping others. He had never so much as put a plaster on the cut finger of a child. They fended for themselves from a very early age – it was meant to be character building. As such, he had no idea whatsoever of how to help the witch. He could only cradle her head in his lap and wait. Puddlebrain's breathing was shallow, her face pale. He ignored the feelings of self contempt at actually caring. It wasn't gnomish. Well, he would just have to pick and choose the aspects of his race that he wanted to adopt. No one was here to judge except he, himself – and he wasn't going to tell anyone.

Billy looked around nervously. He was expecting silence in the forest. At first he thought silence would have been terrifying, but now he thought it would be quite nice. Whistles, twits, creaks and groans echoed around him, taunting him. The sounds snatched at his ears like rats at a corpse. The Grimace was hungry and Billy was food. He could see outside, beyond the trees into the Field. It was like looking through fog. Little Whimsy was shrouded, it seemed, in a mist that shifted and blurred. He knew the mist was only the edge of the woods and didn't extend to the town. It was a sort of barrier, one they should have heeded. He would have very much liked to still be on the other side.

Why was he kneeling here? Why was he holding the unconscious head of a witch? Why had he even entered the forest? He was always telling himself, and anyone within earshot, that he was a gnome! Gnomes didn't just do that! It was, he thought, a good job he was an exile. If word got back to Templemead of his distinctly un-gnomish behaviour, he'd most definitely be kicked out. But he couldn't leave her. She needed him, and that was something alien to a gnome. Gnomes needed no one and no one needed them. Except Puddlebrain. And her sisters. And the rest of Little Whimsy. It was awakening disturbing sensations within Billy – disturbing in that he quite liked them. He couldn't go. He wasn't even sure if the Grimace would let him leave.

So he knelt there, Puddlebrain's head in his lap, the twilight of the woods descending past dusk into night. The noises quietened to a whisper, something that only served to increase their sinister feel. The trees seemed to lean in closer, waiting for Billy's attention to wander or for him to fall asleep so they could pounce. He had tried patting Puddlebrain's cheeks to rouse her. It didn't work. Shaking her was futile too. She was barely breathing and the gnome had to keep putting his ear to her mouth to make sure she was still alive.

"Come on witch!" he hissed. "Wake up!"

But nothing worked. After a while he drifted off to sleep. It happened before he'd realised. Had he been given a chance, he would have fought to stay awake. He would have slapped himself to stop his eyelids becoming heavy. He would have bitten his tongue to stop the yawning and stretching he didn't know he was doing. Was it the forest's doing? Were the trees deliberately making that soft, rhythmic swishing sound to lull him into a slumber? Or was it the energy and excitement of the day taking its toll? Either way, Billy was soon snoring softly. Normally gnomes snored like erupting volcanoes, the sound was often loud enough to wake neighbours in the next street, but here it seemed even his snoring was afraid to make too much noise.

Chapter Twenty Four

Billy yawned. His jaw cracked and his neck cricked as he opened his eyes, rubbing them with his fists. His legs were numb, bent under his body with something heavy lying across them. What? Where?

Oh.

The tiredness left the gnome in an instant, fleeing as he remembered where he was. He looked down at Puddlebrain. She was stirring, finally.

"Puddlebrain," Billy whispered. "Puddlebrain! Wake up."

It was one of the few times he used the witches' names. Normally he addressed them as 'Witch' or 'Hey You', which was fine as that was what they expected. Niceties were nonentities as far as their guest was concerned. Here, though, even the gnome felt the need for a sense of closeness.

Puddlebrain moaned softly and her eyelids fluttered open. "What happened?" she croaked.

"You fainted or something."

"Fainted? How?"

"How? How does a person normally faint? You collapsed unconscious in a heap on the ground. As graceful as a ballet dancing brick. Isn't that the usual way?"

Billy couldn't help the need to carry on being a gnome, at least a pretence was better than nothing.

Puddlebrain pushed herself up and turned to face him. She moved slowly, stiffly, her teeth clenched. She stretched her arms and legs to ease the aches caused from lying across the roots of the oak. She looked at him without saying anything, contemplating a jibe or two in response to his comments, but she knew it was pointless. He was a gnome. As such she supposed he didn't do too bad. She could forgive him his little idiosyncrasies. So she took a deep breath.

"How long have I been out of it?" she asked.

"Hours," Billy said, not bothering to mention that he'd been asleep himself. "I tried everything to wake you up, but nothing worked. All I could do was protect you until you woke up."

Protect her? Well, not quite. Sitting with her and snoozing was a loose definition of the word and not one that would have deterred attackers, but she didn't know that.

"Has anything happened? Have you seen anything?"

"Nothing but trees and darkness." Billy shook his head. "There were some weird noises a while ago, but they've faded now. It's just you, me and the night. Cosy, eh?"

"Very." Puddlebrain went to stand up, but her stiff joints made sure she regretted it. She winced. "Help me up, please."

Billy gave the witch his shoulder to lean on as she pushed herself upright. It was the best he could do in light of his small stature. Puddlebrain groaned as she flexed her limbs and jumped on the spot to kick her circulation into gear.

"Thanks," she said.

"Pleasure," Billy replied. "Now what?"

Puddlebrain looked around. She couldn't see out of the forest at all. It wasn't simply that it was dark, it seemed that the forest was *hiding* the outside world from them. She should at least have been able to see the odd light in a window out over the Field in Little Whimsy, but there was nothing. Then she remembered. There was probably no one left to burn a light. She turned her attention inwards.

The Grimace was featureless. The night was a blanket that wiped clean any distinguishing marks left behind by the taint of day. Yes, there were trees, a great many mighty oaks, but there were so many as to make them blend into each other, one becoming impossible to tell apart from its neighbour. That it would be extremely easy for them to become lost in here was plainly obvious. That there didn't seem to be any sort of path, natural or otherwise was also obvious. It meant there was little point trying to discern a direction to go in. It was a case of walk the way you were facing. So that's what they did.

"Thataway!" Puddlebrain exclaimed.

She started off, her back to the Field, her front to the darkness. Billy paused for a moment, contemplating running, staying or crumbling up into a ball, then went after her, running to catch up.

"Where are we going?" he asked once he was by her side.

"In." she said confidently, which, of course, she wasn't. "We're going in."

"Sounds like a plan," Billy mumbled.

It actually sounded like insanity, but he decided the whole day had been pretty much insane by now. A little more dippedy-do wouldn't really hurt. Or it wouldn't if they weren't on their way into the heart of the Grimace…

The pair strode, tripped and stumbled their way through the trees. Clear paths were suddenly a maze of tangled roots that wrapped around their ankles or appeared in front of their shins just in time to be walked into. Branches that were originally high above their heads abruptly snarled in their hair or swiped at their cheeks. They continued on regardless, but it soon became evident that the Grimace was trying to stop them. If they turned one way, a knot of vines threatened to catch them in its web. If they turned another, the trunks of the oaks were impossibly close, creating a wall they had no hope of breaching. Finally, if they turned back, the darkness was so absolute, it looked as if the world they had just left had disappeared. They were trapped, penned in like goats, the Grimace their shepherd.

"We're trapped," said Puddlebrain quietly.

"Oh?" said Billy. "And there's me thinking this was a barn dance."

"Do you have any suggestions?" she asked. "Instead of just making sarcastic comments, you could try being constructive for a change."

"Constructive?" Billy exclaimed. "How's this? We shouldn't be here. We should have stayed at home. We should be having dinner!"

Puddlebrain grabbed the gnome by the front of his tunic. She pulled him close, face to face. His legs dangled in mid air as she lifted him off the ground.

"Constructive, gnome, means helpful. You are as much a part of this as I am. You decided to plant yourself in our back garden, we didn't ask you. If it's your home, then that makes you part of our family, so we are in this TOGETHER!" She leaned in closer so their noses were touching. She ignored his fetid breath and, through gritted teeth, said: "Now get a grip and try and help!"

She let go of the gnome and he fell to the floor with a dull thump. Billy sat, stunned. Where was the real Puddlebrain? Who was this mad woman? What was…? Hold on. She said he was part of her family…?

Erm…

Billy was lost for words, a rare novelty. To a gnome, family was simply the people you couldn't choose to be without. It was none of this stand up for each other and *like* one another rubbish that everyone seemed to be hung up on. Billy was in immediate danger of actually being nice and wanting to be, and he wasn't sure he wanted to be. But he wasn't sure he didn't want to be. And Billy wasn't sure he could help himself either way. He stood up slowly, brushing himself down. He stared at the witch, not knowing what to say or do – something else he wasn't used to.

Deep breath.

"You're a witch, right?"

Puddlebrain frowned.

"Yes…" she said slowly. "And…?"

"Then *witch!*" Billy waved his hand manically at the trees in example. "Blast them out of the way or something!"

Puddlebrain lifted her hands and looked at her fingers. It had been a long time. A very long time. Could she? Would it work? The thing was, she wasn't Billy or Edna or even Gemini. She wasn't a blaster. She couldn't just destroy things. She liked to make things, to heal and create. Besides, she was friends with nature. It sounded like a cliché when she said it to herself, but it was true, as most clichés were. Puddlebrain liked nature and nature quite liked her too. The rain would only wet her when she wanted to be wet. Grass would grow around her when she wanted to lose herself. Animals and birds would chat with her and all of this was without her powers. Now she had them back, she couldn't turn on her friends. There had to be another way.

Chapter Twenty Five

"There's got to be another way, Billy," she said quietly, her hands dropping to her sides. "I won't destroy them."

"*Won't...?*"

Billy jumped up and down in frustration. Any other time the sight of the gnome performing what looked like a sulk dance might have been funny. Here, they had left fun back home. He slammed his feet down onto the ground and faced Puddlebrain.

"You won't? Do you know what is at stake here? Your sisters! You don't want to hurt a few deformed trees in order to save your *sisters?* What is wrong with you, girl!"

Puddlebrain had had enough. She had put up with the gnome and his moods and his comments for long enough. Ever since he'd planted himself in their back garden, she's been subject to his cutting, so-called jokes. No more. She stepped forward suddenly, a move that surprised Billy and made him fall backwards.

"Deformed? You, a gnome, talks about being deformed? Look at that hump on your back! Look at that excuse for a nose! Destroy! Blast! Maim! Is that all you are interested in? What if there's a better way? What if we can do this quietly? Peacefully? What then? Hurt for the *sake* of it? Because it's easy?"

"No! Because it's fast! Look around you witch!" Billy gestured wildly at the trees. "We are in the Grimace! We are trapped! There *is* no other way! They are only trees! They don't matter! Now stop being a stupid little girl and just *do it!*"

Right.

Puddlebrain drew in a slow breath through tightly clenched teeth. She let it out through her nose, a faint whistling disturbing the silence that had slammed down like a hammer between them. She was *not* stupid. She left that to Gemini, who managed it so well. She was *not* a little girl and hadn't been for a very long time. She was over three hundred and fifty years old! When would people start treating her like it? She had outlived the entire population of Little Whimsy many times over and still they thought of her as a youngster. Now this gnome, who knew little more than how to hurl abuse, had joined in the fray? She wasn't going to stand for it, not any more. She was tired of being the brunt of insults and jokes. She was completely fed up with being the baby of the family - of the town in fact. It had to stop, and it would stop right here and right now.

She raised her hand slowly.

"Finally!" Billy exclaimed, pushing himself up.

She pointed it at the gnome.

"Wha…?" Billy looked amazed. He couldn't understand what he was seeing. Why would she be aiming at him? They were friends! "You can't! You need…"

She flicked.

The gnome froze as the magic enveloped him in a silvery web. Strands of light sped over his body as if a hundred invisible spiders were wrapping him in their silks. A low moan escaped his lips as his body started to creak and bend, making him sound like an old rocking chair pitching to and fro. There was a ripping sound and his shoes began to swell and split, the seams bursting apart. Billy's toes were growing longer, stretching and changing colour to a deep terracotta brown. The tips of his toes bent suddenly downwards and plunged into the earth, splitting and spreading. His body scrunched and twisted. His arms were forced upwards and outwards, his fingers lengthening and splitting apart like his toes had.

His face, already gnarled, solidified, the colour changing from grey, like the sky when it's deciding whether or not to rain, to match his feet and his arms and hands. His eyes became small knot holes. Tiny leaves budded at the extremities of his fingertips. His ears, normally large and flappy, became dark bores, the sort you'd expect a squirrel to poke its head out of.

In seconds the transformation was done. Billy was no longer a gnome. He had become one of the trees he so bitterly wanted destroyed.

Puddlebrain was shaking. She felt guilty. She hadn't wanted to hurt him, but she had no choice. Besides, he wasn't hurt, only… changed. It was his own fault. What could she do? How could she concentrate on helping her sisters and everyone else when he was constantly making jibes and insults and everything? Dragging her down and stamping on her emotions?

Puddlebrain sighed. She turned around to face the heart of the Grimace realising that she was now on her own. Billy had been noisy and he had been a pain, but at least he had been *there*. No matter. What was done was done and there was only one option. Puddlebrain had to continue alone. She breathed in deeply, letting it out slowly.

Calm. Be calm. Focus.

In a little while, she felt better. Billy had been a help, but he'd also been a distraction. She may very well need him in the near future – she had no idea what she might face – but she couldn't be doing with the agitation the gnome couldn't help but cause. This was the only way, and she was sure it was the right way.

But still…

Puddlebrain looked around, wondering which way she could go. The Grimace hung over and about her, hemming her in. She could hear its laughter in the whisper of the breeze through the leaves. It taunted her, taking the gnome's lead.

Well, she thought, *the joke's over.*

"Now then," she said matter-of-factly to the air. "Let's stop this nonsense. I haven't come here to hurt you, nor have I come to play games. The fact is, I need to get through you to whatever it is I'm heading for, and I could do with some help. If you can't manage that, but you're not hindering me, I suppose that's the next best thing. How about it?"

The air, the trees, the forest ignored her. They were eternal, or at least very nearly. They had been there for longer than even they could remember and would be so far into the future. Who was this girl to intrude and test their patience? Who was she to command them? No. Hurt them? Hah! They would keep her there, trapped. It would be her penance for the intrusion. Already they tired of even noticing she existed and so ignored her pleas. The patience of an oak is as mighty as the tree itself. Time is meaningless to something that could potentially last forever, so the comings and goings of mortals and their world were nothing to the Grimace. Time had granted them an arrogance that came to match their warped stature. They were the *Grimace.* Nothing else mattered.

"Come *on*," pleaded Puddlebrain, knowing as she spoke that it was no use.

She could sense the indifference of the forest. She knew it didn't care for her problems. She could almost taste the ages soaked into the trunks of the oaks, like water into a sponge, and suddenly felt very small. She was a girl. Hardly a witch at all, especially as she'd only just regained her magic. The Grimace was the *Grimace.* What was she in comparison to that? She was the blink of an eye to them, the buzz of an insect that irritated for a second and then was gone. If she reached out to stroke the bark she could probably feel the years infused therein.

No!

Puddlebrain snatched her hand back! She was a hair's breadth away from touching one of the trees. Without even been aware that she was doing so, she seemed to have somehow been lulled into a trance. It had happened so quickly and so completely she didn't get the chance to feel it overcoming her. What might have happened if she *had* touched the tree, she didn't know. Perhaps nothing, but perhaps…

Was the forest conspiring against her? She looked again at Billy. Had she been too harsh? Could she have been a shiver away from becoming just like him?

"Right," she said. "I did ask first. Remember that"

Chapter Twenty Six

'Witches are as witches do,' her mother once told her when she was very young.

At the time, Puddlebrain had no idea what her mother had been waffling on about. Way back then it hadn't mattered – her mother was very sweet, but had a tendency to be eccentric sometimes. Puddlebrain, indeed the three sisters together, listened to their mother's words and just nodded their collective heads, even if it didn't make any sense. The phrase still didn't entirely mean anything, but Puddlebrain had a idea of what her mother was trying to say. She was a witch. Act like one.

Of course, that depended on what sort of witch you were. Edna was used to people doing as she said so she would simply blunder in. She wouldn't bother to ask questions as she often believed she already knew the answers. Gemini, bless her, was a meat pie short of a Sunday dinner, so she blundered in too, but really because she didn't think about things properly. For her, there were no questions and who cared about answers? It was almost thirteen o'clock and she was hungry!

Puddlebrain was like neither of these. She couldn't help but think of the consequences of her actions. If she was forced into doing something she didn't like, as in the case of Billy, she felt guilty afterwards. On many occasions Edna had told her not to be so wet. Puddlebrain couldn't help it. She was *wet*, although she didn't think of it that way. As far as she was concerned, she was considerate. If that made her wet, or even a bit damp, then that was who she was.

So.

Witches are as witches do.

OK, mother.

The forest ignored her. She was nothing and it was mighty. She had been thoughtful and asked nicely. She had done her best to be reasonable in an unreasonable situation.

Puddlebrain raised her hand before her. She wrinkled her brow in concentration. One last chance? Any takers?

The witch knew it was time to be a witch. She extended her finger and slowly swirled it around, pointing all the while at the trees that kept her a prisoner. At first there was no reaction. The Grimace, stalwart and resolute, thought as little of her magic as it did of her.

She stretched her hand out further, the spinning finger rotating faster. A whirlpool of light, all sparkles and dust, drifted in the wake of her fingertip. It spiralled, looking like one of the fireworks let off during the Grand Festival of Summer, which, for some strange reason, was always held in autumn. The wisps of light began to extend forward from her hand, the whirl straightening into a stretched coil. Like tendrils of electricity, a phenomenon yet to reach the village of Little Whimsy (although some of the larger towns and cities apparently used it), the magic that Puddlebrain was conjuring danced from branch to trunk to leaf to root, an almost passionate waltz of enchantment that belied the motives beneath. Pausing to dip only past the fossilised gnome, she turned about, casting a wide circle of light in the otherwise darkened forest. She clenched her teeth. Sweat popped onto her face and ran down her cheeks like juice from a freshly bitten apple. Still there was nothing.

Wait…

A low groaning sound seemed to rumble from the floor of the Grimace. It vibrated up through Puddlebrain's legs, making her clenched teeth feel like they were being pulsed out of her head. The Grimace was waking up to the fact that, this time, they could not ignore the intruder in their midst. Puddlebrain raised her other hand and splayed all her fingers out wide. She had never done anything like this before, but was tearing a page from her sisters' book. She wasn't thinking. Until then, a simple hand movement and a little concentration had been all that was needed to cast a spell. Now, however, Puddlebrain was using her entire body. The Grimace was, truly, mighty, but they hadn't counted on a little witch with a big attitude.

With both arms outspread, still turning, the witch began to move her lips, chanting a spell that went unheard through the steadily growing growl of the forest. Her voice may have been unheard, but the effects certainly were not. With a languor that seemed as if the forest was moving in slow motion, the trees began to straighten. The intertwined branches moved upwards, away from each other, separating the trees from being a mass, almost a single body, to being individuals. Twigs and leaves flattened against the larger branches. Some snapped when the force of being bent, with the tree itself fighting the transformation, was too much for the lesser boughs. Snaps and cracks echoed around her, the cries of the forest, sounding like some massive beast stampeding towards her. Still the trees bent upwards, reaching for the sky, desperate for the sunlight, or at this time of night, moonlight, that had been denied them for so long. As they reached, so the blanket of leaves above Puddlebrain thinned.

The moon was a sliver away from being full. The sky was cloudless and the stars shone almost as bright as the moon. The way forward, until now barred from the witch, had been opened. A small, tight pathway led further into the forest, a little too invitingly. Puddlebrain stopped turning and lowered her arms. She wiped the sweat from her brow with her sleeve. She frowned. How? Where?

"What do you…?" Puddlebrain paused.

She had been about to ask Billy what he thought about the path. Naturally, being a tree himself (or unnaturally in this case), he couldn't answer. She wondered suddenly if he could still hear her.

"Billy, I'm sorry. It had to be done. I don't know if you can hear me, or if you believe me, but it was for the best. I didn't know what else to do. I needed help, not…" She searched for a word other than whinging, but couldn't think of one. "I've got to go," she said finally. "Wish me luck."

Puddlebrain turned to face the path. *Careful*, she told herself. She wasn't entirely sure how the pathway had appeared. She was sure she had simply caused an opening – made the trees part to allow her to pass. Her spell had been more of a show of strength to the Grimace than anything else. She wanted it to know her. She wanted it to understand that she had to get though with or without its help.

But how, exactly?

She was a witch, but she was a simple one at best. Neither her nor her sisters had ever conjured the sort of power that had been needed to bend a forest – a mean, dark and menacing forest – to their will. They could do almost anything they wanted, indeed, but the Grimace had power of its own. Not magic, perhaps, but it had an indomitable force of will if nothing else. She knew that, if she had thought about how to conquer that will, she probably wouldn't have managed to do so.

She could turn a gnome into a tree. She could dance in the rain and not get wet. She could do so many things, but this was beyond her experience. That frightened her. All of a sudden it seemed she was more than she should be. She had to keep that under control, but wasn't sure she could do so. She had intended on pushing the trees aside. That was it. Instead she had forced them to embrace the sky. That wasn't in their nature. The Grimace was shadowy. It was brooding. It embraced nothing except the night. She had changed that.

Had it changed her?

This was getting her nowhere. Time and again she found herself worrying about what had and what might happen. She was dwelling too much and doing too little. Thoughts swept over her without warning, carrying the witch away on their currents. She had to fight to keep her feet and her focus.

But she was only a girl! She was the baby! She was…

Puddlebrain slapped her forehead. It was the Grimace! It was stealing her away from herself. The Grimace was the current that swept her along, not her own thoughts. She smiled bitterly.

Thought you had me there. I'll show you.

Still unsure of the pathway – had she created it or was it the Grimace's doing? – Puddlebrain knew she had no choice. If she stayed, she would achieve nothing except be seduced by the forest into either forgetting herself or wallowing in her unnecessary feelings of guilt. She walked to the start of the path. Tall, thick oaks lined its edges. She could feel them staring down at her, waiting for their chance. Well they could wait!

Boldly, Puddlebrain slapped her hand onto the trunk of the nearest one. It was rough and cold, but she could instantly feel the energy rumbling within. She was aware of the creeping sensation that seemed to crawl up her arm from her fingertips, but ignored it. *She* was telling the *forest*, not the other way around. She furrowed her brow, pursed her lips and pushed. She held her hand there, hard against the trunk, for a few long seconds while sparks of her magic spat at the wood. When she finally pulled her hand away, there was a print on the tree like the shadow of her hand that had forgotten it was meant to move with her, or had maybe fallen asleep and needed to be woken, an afterimage left behind to say 'Hey! This is ME! Don't you forget it!"

Puddlebrain nodded, satisfied. She hadn't needed to do much, just enough to leave her mark. She stepped onto the pathway and started along it.

Chapter Twenty Seven

Little Whimsy echoed.

The wind whipped along the streets with a brisk energy as if the absence of any residents was the chance for it to party like children left to their own devices while their parents were away. It lashed at bushes and grass, flaying along with the mood of teenagers bored with school holidays, finding distraction in making noise.

It echoed.

Along avenues where the wind hadn't yet reached with its festivities, no-one walked. No cats slept, no dogs watered hedgerows, and no women gossiped. Mrs. Mead's ovens were empty, and the air smelled of lavender from the bush outside her kitchen window. Mrs. Mead's own little pocket of air never usually smelled of anything but pie. With no people to soak up the silence with their bustle, Little Whimsy seemed to resonate like the inside of Lem Artthorpe's head, empty of everything except a few stale old memories and a dusty lump that might once have been a kind contemplation.

The school building was akin to a baby's rattle without the rattle bit that rattled around inside. It was silent of the shouts and the laughter and the thrum of thought. It didn't whisper of pencil on paper or scratch of chalk on board. Young Prefect Waddle hadn't donged the school bell that morning in Mr. Bopsidy's absence due to the fact that young Prefect Waddle was absent himself. This would have been surprising in itself if it wasn't neatly tied up with the fact that everyone else was absent as well.

And not just at the school. Every one of Little Whimsy's inhabitants would have been given a red mark for attendance, or lack of, if anyone had happened to be around to mark a register.

Ghost towns.

Part myth, part fact, the two having danced together for so long it was impossible to see which was real and what was fable. Upper Falstead was a ghost town. No one in Little Whimsy knew where either Upper or Lower, or Middle for that matter, Falstead was. They didn't care to visit so it didn't really matter, but they knew the stories right enough. Tales of headless men who walked the streets at night. Dogs with red eyes and dripping teeth. Women, dressed in grand gowns of years gone by, but each with their… Well, they were not tales to tell their children at night, or to tell each other by day.

One man had caused this. One man, devoid of reasoning and care, had reduced a thriving community to a horrific legend that made even grown men shudder if they so much as heard the name. That man, Edward Hulme, was long dust in the ground, but his name lived on, a dry taste in the throat. And the town of Upper Falstead lived on, after a fashion, in his wake. Whether the stories of the dead walking and devil-eyed dogs were true or not wasn't an issue. The town of Upper Falstead, just north of Lower and a little east and up-a-bit from Middle, was what they called in the trade (whichever trade dealt with such things), a ghost town. Nobody living ambled along its avenues.

Possibly, the dead did though…

The same feeling of unspoken menace and keep-looking-over-your-shoulder-dread slithered along the streets of Little Whimsy. It was an invisible snake, coiling and uncoiling, forked tongue flicking like a dagger in the eye, ready to snap at any who might be foolish enough to pass by. Of course that wasn't going to happen. There was no one around, foolish or otherwise. Little Whimsy might not have the terrible celebrity of Upper Falstead, but it felt as if it *should* have. There might not be rabid dogs, hungry for a bite of leg or a mouthful of arm, hiding around every corner, but there *could* have been. There was an unnatural chill in the air, one that wasn't in keeping with the clear sky and bright sun that had been the norm the past few days.

Through the night, a shadow moved. It was a ripple of darkness and it was searching. Casting about, seemingly in all directions at once, it didn't hide or sneak. It was confident and proud and it knew it was alone. It knew it wouldn't be challenged – not that any such confrontation would do any good. How could you fight something that wasn't really there? How could a battle be won against a creature as insubstantial as the darkness it emulated?

It was a thief. It had stolen the inhabitants of Little Whimsy. It had taken the life out of the town coldly and simply. There was no feeling, no empathy, no sense of anything but a dark purpose.

But the shadow *knew* it was alone, and it was troubled. Its indecision played across its surface like the wind across a lake – whips and snatches of darkness sweeping across the otherwise featureless black. There should have been more – two more. One wasn't imperative, it was merely the last of the villagers, the finale to a glorious day. The other, though, was different. It had to find that one. It must! That one was different. That one was important. That one was the *key*.

The echoes of Little Whimsy avoided the shadow. They knew that to touch it was to be as dead as the village. They ricocheted about the streets almost desperate to create some noise in the barren town. The shadow would steal that, too, if it could.

The gate at the back to the witches' house shook in tight vibrations that it struggled to keep under control. It was trying, so hard, to stay closed. The *thing* that stood near shouldn't be allowed entry, the gate knew. The witches' had entrusted it with security and it knew its duty. But the gate was merely wood held together by a few screws. It could do its best, but it wasn't sure that would be enough. It was afraid.

The shadow hovered for a few moments, searching. It had no senses of taste or touch, but it could still feel, after a fashion. It knew the one it sought had been here. The sensation was strong. In its own way, the shadow could smell her, could taste her energy. It knew this was the one, having taken two like her already. But *this* one! This one indeed. The prize. The *key!*

It had already ventured into this building without issue when it had taken the other two so the gates feeble attempts were almost laughable. But the trail led off away from the house. Towards the field. Towards the dark trees? Towards the Entrance perhaps?

The shadow, all black ripples and liquid night, started off, following a path that only it could see. It travelled slowly, deliberately. It could have simply appeared at the other end of this trail and be on its prey before they knew it, but it wanted to savour the chase. It couldn't lose them – her - now. There was no rush. The sun wouldn't rise for hours yet, then Halloween would reign. Not costumey, trick-or-treaty, kiddified Halloween, but HALLOWEEN!

A faint cackle drifted from the shadow, which was picked up by the breeze, and dropped as quickly. Even the wind wanted nothing to do with *it.*

Chapter Twenty Eight

Puddlebrain had started along the pathway. She knew, as she walked slowly forward, that this was not of her doing. The trees were leering over her, their branches softly rustling, letting her know she wasn't forgotten. The Grimace had made this path. Perhaps it was in part due to the magic she'd shown the forest. Maybe it was giving in, submitting to what it saw of her power. She thought it was probably more the fact that, if it couldn't get rid of her, the Grimace would guide her to where it wanted her to go. She just hoped that she needed to go the same way.

Once, she looked back the way she had come. The forest had closed behind her. Indeed, the path was disappearing almost as soon as her feet had moved forward. She was virtually being pushed forward, the Grimace forcing a sense of urgency upon the witch.

"Come on," it was saying. "Get a move on!"

She had no choice but to walk faster, lest her ankles be snapped at by the over-zealous roots of the Grimace. But get a move on to what? To where? Puddlebrain was sure she'd find out soon enough and she hoped she was prepared for it.

It was dark.

Her eyes had, to a certain extent, become accustomed to the lack of light, but she still had to feel her way along. The pathway was fast becoming a sliver between the trees. With it closing up behind her, she had no time to stop and think or to use her magic to either brighten her way or widen the passage ahead. The branches above were interlocked like the knuckles of a pair of giant hands preparing to close in and squash her in their fist. They squeezed out any light from the night sky making everything seem like shadow layered upon shadow, thick and threatening, larger than life and infinitely more dangerous.

Puddlebrain wasn't normally a claustrophobic person, Gemini had the prize for that one, but she could understand how her sister might feel. More than once she tripped and fell, picking herself up only just in time to avoid being consumed by the rapidly fusing forest. Before long she was running, the permanent dusk making her feel almost blind. Branches whipped at her face, snagging her hair, tearing at her clothes.

She stumbled again and this time caught her breath as she heard, close by, a grumble of low laughter. She stared about frantically.

Was that a pair of red eyes, slashing the night?

Too quick to be sure, the harsh crimson rips were gone. But she was sure they had been there, wasn't she? And the laughter? A growl that crawled along the inside of the skin on her forearms? Had she really heard it? Or was it just the Grimace playing games with her? Puddlebrain was facing back the way she had come. The path had vanished, becoming a blanket of colourless branches and leaves that wrapped the night in indistinct detail. She was panting, drawing the air in through rapid, hoarse gasps. She couldn't move. The strength had been drained from her as easily as if she'd been a wet rag, rung out before being pegged on a line to dry. Her head hung forward and her eyes were closed. She struggled to control her breathing and her heaving chest.

"Come on," she told herself. "*Come on*. Calm. Be calm."

She opened her eyes. The forest was silent around her, waiting for her next move. Puddlebrain frowned. Why hadn't the forest closed upon her completely, drowning her in its foliage, consuming her like a spider does a fly? What was it waiting for? After a quick glance behind her to check the pathway was still open, she shuffled backwards on her bottom. As she moved, there was a hushed creaking as roots slid through the mud and branches stretched over to close the path where she had just been. She stopped moving, and the forest stopped closing.

Puddlebrain tilted her head to one side in thought. She drew her foot towards her slowly, and a root, as thick as her wrist and as long as her arm, slithered, snakelike, into the gap she had just created. She stretched her leg back out, but the root continued to uncoil, followed closely by a spindly branch covered in anaemic yellowing leaves. She retreated a little more, and again the Grimace reclaimed its territory.

Shuffle, close, stop. Shuffle, close stop.

The forest was playing with her. She felt like a child's doll, pulled and pushed as the Grimace saw fit. It was dancing, with her an unwilling partner, in a tuneless tango. She would *not* play this game! She would *not* bop this boogie, as Gemini might say.

Puddlebrain stood up. She smiled at the trees around her, wondering how they would feel if this particular toy chose not to play. Well, let's find out, eh? Let's dance to a different beat.

So. Here was she, a witch. Here were trees. Perfect. A match made in magic. Puddlebrain reached out and took hold of a particularly smooth branch. Glancing around her, sure the forest was just holding its breath, waiting for the chance to pounce, she tried to snap the branch off. The tree she was pulling at was resisting. She could feel it through her hands. It tensed as she pulled and she didn't quite have the strength to break it off.

Hey, never mind! There were more ways, she knew, to boil a broth than simply lighting a match. Holding the branch firmly in one hand, the witch reached out with her other hand and lightly touched where it joined the trunk. There was a crunchy slicing noise, sounding just like a knife cutting through a lettuce, and the branch came away from the tree in a clean break. The tree, one of the few elms that had managed to survive amongst the overpowering oaks, flailed its branches as if in pain and anger. It whipped out at Puddlebrain's head, but she easily managed to avoid being hit.

"Oh, hush now," she smiled. "You'll only go and grow another one. Besides, you've got dozens more. You won't miss this little one here!"

She confidently turned her back on the elm and ran her hand along the length of the branch, humming softly. The leaves and twigs and offshoots sprouting from it fell away leaving an unmarked main stem that glistened faintly with residual magic. Puddlebrain inspected it and nodded to herself. Good choice. She suddenly felt, rather than heard, the Grimace drawing in its breath, probably in response to her damaging one of its own. She'd expected this, and was ready. Quickly pushed one end of the branch against the earth, the witch swung her leg astride it. She looked back and saw the trees reaching towards her, clawing the air. She waited until they were a whisper away and then kicked at the ground.

"Catch me if you can!" she cried…

…And took off! Her feet left the floor and the branch, now smooth and sleek as if carved and polished by the finest broomstick craftsman in town (there were no broomstick craftsmen in town, they all live in Upper Witherton, but if there *was* one…), swept along the path more than twice as fast as Puddlebrain could have run. She leaned forwards, almost hugging the shaft, giving as little as possible to the forest's claws. The limbs of the oaks closed on empty air and the forest tried to gather about her, but it was simply not fast enough.

Having lived for so long, it was used to everything happening at a lingering pace. It wasn't prepared for this rush of a girl. She'd disrupted its slumber and it had tried to teach her, but she hadn't learned the lesson. She hadn't *wanted* to learn!

Well then.

The Grimace shook itself, a shiver that ran through the leaves of every bush, oak and sliver of grass. It still chased the witch along the path created for her, but knew it couldn't catch up. Still, it wanted her to think it was trying. There were more ways, it knew, to catch a mouse than to simply buy a cat. Of course it didn't know this literally, it was a forest, and forests knew nothing of commerce or the eternal power struggle between feline and rodent, but it had the *essence* of the idea. And the Grimace realised that, if this intruder was watching her back, she would be less likely to be watching where she was headed.

The path led her on and she followed it without a thought as to where it might end. Even after so many years of not being able to fly, she was still adept. She assumed that this was what 'ordinary' people meant when they talked about 'as easy as riding a bicycle'. She had always been an acrobatic flyer, preferring to test her brooms and her talents to their limit – none of this 'As long as it gets me from here to there, I'm happy' nonsense that her sisters spouted. She wanted to fly the highest, swoop the fastest, and get as many loops in as she could along the way.

So Puddlebrain knew her business. She and her broomstick were almost a part of each other as they swept through the Grimace ducking and swaying and dodging along the path. Branches whipped as is they had every intention of taking her head clean off, but she avoided them effortlessly. Roots reached out like gnarled tentacles, wanting to grab her ankles and yank her back, but she out-flew them easily. A blur, she raced onwards, leaving the looming forest behind.

Flying was one of Puddlebrain's talents, of that there was no doubt. Unfortunately, she had never quite managed to perfect the tricky art of stopping sharply.

Chapter Twenty Nine

One moment she was surrounded by a host of oaks desperate to rip her to pieces, the next she was in a huge clearing almost bereft of any greenery at all. She gasped and instinctively let go of the broomstick. The front end dipped suddenly and grazed the floor, flipping the witch. She flew through the air, unaided this time, and landed flat on her back on a sparsely grassed stretch of hard mud.

Winded and bruised, Puddlebrain laid there, her ears ringing like the church belfry on a Sunday morning. She tried to sit up but couldn't. She tried to move more than her arms, but she couldn't, and even moving those was painful. She wheezed, drawing her breaths in as if through a wad of cloth, it was so difficult. Her head ached from being slammed into the hard mud. She groaned, and the groan turned into a cough that threatened to burst her throat apart.

Her broomstick had recovered from its own tumble and drifted hesitantly over to the witch. It had only just met her, a brief introduction that had been so swift it hadn't even included a hello. There was no "Hi, I'm a witch" – "Hi, I'm a branch." It was simply a jump on and go!

And then this had happened.

The broomstick knew it wasn't at fault. It hadn't really had any choice in the direction or speed they'd been flying – the witch had been in total control, although perhaps 'control' was a little too strong a term considering… Still. She *had* removed it from the Grimace. She *had* taken it from the elm that had given it birth. In doing so, and in giving it the gift of flight, she had made the former branch feel as if it was waking up from a drugged sleep, not that it particularly knew what drugs or sleep were. Being a part of the Grimace was overpowering and smothering, and you knew nothing else other than the feeling of being overpoweringly smothered. It was normal. It was natural. To be separated from that was… enlightening. Having a sense of self was new and, well, wondrous! And it was thanks to this witch! The broomstick nudged her.

You ok?

Puddlebrain tried to push her creation away. She was decidedly *not* ok. She had bruised her pride and her back and could do without any creeping concern from the scabby bit of wood that had thrown her! The effort of lifting her arm was too much for her and she flopped it back down, wincing as it hit the ground. Again the broomstick nudged her, this time more insistently. She turned her head towards it a little too sharply.

"What!?"

The broomstick backed off but stayed close. It was hovering a few centimetres off the ground, swaying slightly from side to side. It wasn't quite used to being able to fly, so it was taking things steadily, not wanting to rush or try anything too rash. The race through the Grimace had been enough! It jabbed at the air in a pointing motion. Puddlebrain frowned. What? The broomstick jabbed again. It was definitely pointing. Puddlebrain turned her head stiffly in the direction her broom was indicating.

She sat up abruptly, immediately forgetting her pains.

She was in the centre of the Grimace. It couldn't be anywhere else. Three oaks, so huge they dwarfed even the mighty ones that had made a grab for her on her journey in, formed a triangle in the middle of which she was sprawled. The Grimace ringed the behemoths like an audience waiting to see some spectacular gladiatorial display, or perhaps to simply stare in awe.

She craned her neck back to try to see the tops, but they were lost in the night sky. How these could not be seen from outside the Grimace was beyond the witch. They were blatantly *massive*! Minimal roots could be seen at their bases, as if they'd burrowed deep into the ground for stability and pulled the bodies part way down with them. It gave the trunks the illusion of being moulded from the very ground itself, as if the earth had thrust oak fists skyward. Branches didn't sprout until a good 20 yards up, and the lower ones were easily thicker than Puddlebrain's own torso. Beyond that, she couldn't tell. The upper reaches disappeared into the darkness above. She turned to stare at each colossus, speechless.

Then she saw the marks.

Carved out of the bases of the monsters were concave sections. Not too big, but big enough. They hardly dented the enormous trunks, but they were there, nonetheless. Puddlebrain could see that they were quite old now, at least old in her sense. As far as the Grimace was concerned, they had been removed less than a heartbeat ago. She knew what they were. She hoped that the cutting hadn't harmed the trees in any way. This was not only because she didn't want any retaliation aimed at her, but because that's how she was – she would even care for something she feared. But, she supposed, the Grimace wouldn't know she was her father's daughter, would it?

"Not quite," said a voice.

Puddlebrain spun round. Wha…? The broomstick had been pointing. In her awe at the sight of the three great oaks, she'd forgotten that little fact. She remembered it now, quite suddenly, but there was no one in sight. She turned her head slowly, standing as she did so. Her breathing had returned to normal and her aches were forgotten. The broomstick moved closer to her leg, acting so much like a scared puppy that the witch almost petted it.

She stood, holding her breath, hoping to hear breathing other than her own. The forest was as still as she. Her eyes narrowed as she peered into the darkness of the Grimace, trying to see if any of the shadows were moving. Nothing did.

Was it her imagination?

"No, it wasn't," said the voice.

It sounded like parchment being torn slowly by hands that shook with incredible age. It scratched down her back like the claws of a cat worrying the furniture. She shivered.

Leaning against the trunk of one of the oaks was an old man. At least that was what he first looked like. He'd not been there a second before, Puddlebrain was sure, but he was certainly there now. His face was as wrinkled and lined as the bark he was using as a post and his clothes, grey rags that clung to him like an old friend, looked like they hadn't been taken off in at least a good century or two. A hat, paler than his clothes, more the ashen shade of his face, was pulled tight onto the tops of his ears. It was round topped, like a bowler, but the rim hung down lazily, trying to obscure his eyes but not seeming to have the energy. The old man was settled into one of the dips cut by Puddlebrain's father so many years before. He ran his finger up and down over the wood, stroking it lovingly.

"Who are you?" the witch asked, trying to make her voice sound brave.

This was just an old man, probably more lost than she was. Perhaps he was one of the Grimace's victims, doomed to wander its treacherous paths for the rest of his life.

"Who am I?" the old man said. Puddlebrain cringed at the sound of that voice. It rattled out of the old man like the hacked cough of a pneumonic rat. "Who am I indeed? And who are you to ask who am I? In fact, who are any of us? I know, but do you? *Do* you? Do tell!"

Puddlebrain frowned.

"Pardon?"

Was he senile? Was his poor mind as lost as his poorer body?

"Consider yourself pardoned. At least for the ignorance of your youth. Your arrogance is another matter, as is that of your father, and that will have to be dealt with as a separate issue. But for the ignorance of simply being you, consider yourself forgiven."

The old man wheezed as he spoke. He shifted his position slightly and Puddlebrain could hear the creak of his bones from where she was standing.

She was silent. He'd spoken of her father, so he knew who she was. Any pretence was a waste of time now, but surely she wouldn't be punished for her father's actions, not that she precisely knew what those actions were. All Puddlebrain really knew was that her father had ventured into the Grimace decades before and had brought out a grand fireplace that, he said, had been carved from the three oaks at its centre. That was all she had been told.

"Is it now?" the old man said. "Is that really all you were told?"

He stepped away from the trunk, a move that seemed to take forever and was accompanied by the creaking of bones that echoed around Puddlebrain's head. It appeared to join his voice in getting inside her somehow and scratching away from within.

"Are you so sure of that young lady?"

Puddlebrain took a step back as he moved towards her, leaning heavily on a slim gnarled cane of some dark stained wood. Who was he? *What* was he? Perhaps she'd banged her head too hard when she'd been thrown from the broomstick. Maybe that was it. Except her broomstick had seen the man too – it had pointed him out to her. And he knew who she was. And…

…And he was reading her thoughts…

"Ha!" he exclaimed. "Almost, but not quite. Why, you're a bright young thing, aren't you? Clever as clever can be, and just about as brave into the bargain. Why should you be afraid of a little old man like me, eh? Littler than little old you, and older than yourself and your sisters added together and timesed a time or two. Afraid? Scared? Nervous as a cat in a kennel, that's you, isn't it?" He laughed, a jangling clatter that threatened to shake him apart. "But you don't need to be afraid. Not of me…"

Chapter Thirty

Puddlebrain looked around, suddenly aware that threats could threaten from any side. The forest was a mass of grey on black. Anyone or anything could be hiding within its dark embrace. She knew she didn't have time for any of this. Her sisters, and the rest of the villagers, were quite probably dead. But if they weren't…

"If they're not, you're going to rescue them, aren't you, girly? You're going to plough right into you don't know where and do you don't know what."

The old man dropped to the ground. He fell with a complete lack of grace or care and should have hurt his backside with the force of impact. Instead, though, there was a muted *whump*, as if the ground had softened to receive him.

"Big brave impulsive girly that you are."

Puddlebrain took offence at being called 'girly'. So she was young, in witch terms. So what? She'd still lived a lot longer than any of the residents of Little Whimsy!

"Are you so sure of that, girly?" the old man cackled.

I wish you wouldn't do that! Puddlebrain thought angrily.

This was getting on her nerves. She didn't know, and right at that moment didn't care, who this old man was. She needed to get on! She'd wasted enough time sleeping when she should have been searching. The last thing she wanted was to be delayed for longer.

"Oh, tush, tish and cherry tomatoes. You don't know what you're going to do anyway, so doing it earlier or later wouldn't stop it being a great big mystery with lashings of uncertainty piled on for good measure, now would it?"

Puddlebrain moaned softly. She held her head in her hands, feeling helpless. He was right. She simply didn't know what she was to do. She had no idea where she was going. If she could work that out, she still didn't know what she could do once she got there. Playing it by ear just wasn't going to work!

"That's your problem, see?" he said. "You don't have the ears to play it by ear. You'd need to be a Lig or at the very least a Daintyfoot to be able to play anything by ear. You being you, I'd have expected you to play it by *finger!*"

He laughed hysterically at this, a joke so hilarious it seemed the whole forest was joining in. The trees quivered with mirth at the joke. It was one kick in the teeth too many for the witch.

She raised her hand and threw a spell at the old man. She didn't even know exactly which spell it was. She just hurled her finger at him in frustration. She wanted him to *stop!* The magic hit him right in the centre of his chest, a silvery gold swirl that lit up his features briefly. The glow dissipated, and he giggled.

"Do it again!" he cried. "It tickled!"

So she did. She raised both her hands high above her head and, as if crashing them onto the keys of an invisible grand piano, brought them slamming down onto the ground. Sparks leapt from her fingers, threatening to set alight the sparse grass that dotted the ground. The sparks became snakes, four of them, tendrils of silver that slithered to and fro across the hard earth towards the strange man. Once they reached him, the snakes spiralled up his legs, their crackling sounding not unlike hissing. They carried on up his body, weaving across the tired cloth of his muddy grey overcoat, and paused at his face. He opened his mouth slightly, as if taking a breath, and with a sharp snap, the snakes dived in. His head whipped backwards and Puddlebrain thought he was going to fall.

Ha! she thought. *Got you!*

The old man was unsteady for a moment. Puddlebrain could see the spell working inside him. The slithers of magic whirled around in his belly, their glow increasing in brightness so that it could easily be seen through his body and his clothes. Within seconds, his whole body was shimmering as the snakes became a concentrated ball of magic churning about inside him.

Then he burped.

The glow vanished.

He was standing still once more, no longer on the verge of collapsing.

"Yum. Chewy, with a hint of cinnamon!"

Puddlebrain sank to the ground. She slumped forward, resigned. What was she thinking? For the umpteenth-and-then-some time, she realised that she wasn't up to the task she had set herself. This time, however, she didn't think she had the strength to convince herself otherwise. She was feeling as if she was on a wagon with a dodgy wheel being drawn by a horse that had lost its mind three weeks last Thursday. The ride was bumpy and frenetic, and she didn't know if she could hold on for much longer.

"Oh fuddleduddle," said the old man. "Pull yourself together girly! You're worse than the Grimace on a cold Autumn day, desperately trying to hold on to the leaves that it *knows* are going to blow off!"

Puddlebrain stared at him. Who *was* he? Her mind was spiralling and she found it difficult to concentrate on anything, even the him.

"And," said the old man, "will you stop thinking of me as an old man! It's very demeaning, dontcha know. Just because I look like an old man and I sound like an old man, doesn't automatically mean I *am* an old man, now does it? You seem to think you're a witch, mighty and powerful indeed. Have we seen much evidence of that? I think not. You've bewitched an elm sapling into being your friend. A broomstick even. Hooray and lad-de-diddle to you. You convinced a few oaks, minor ones at that, on the outskirts of the Grimace to raise their branches to the sun – in the night. Not exactly great achievements, are they?"

He crackled his rattley cackle.

Puddlebrain sighed. Who *did* she think she was? She'd turned her only ally into a tree! How clever was that? Yes, so Billy was an annoying little pain in the posterior, but he was all she'd had. She toyed absently with a sprig of grass that had managed to push through the harsh earth into the clearing. Twisting it around her fingers, she felt just like that blade. Life was twisting her about its fickle fingers, and it threatened to pluck her at any moment.

"You know," the old man wheezed, "that would be almost poetic if it wasn't pathetic! Pull yourself together girly!"

"WHO *ARE* YOU!" she cried, the words punctuated with sobs. "JUST WHO… who are you?"

"Well then," he said. "Finally, a sensible question."

Chapter Thirty One

His old brain was obviously too befuddled to remember that Puddlebrain had already asked this question, but she simply didn't have the strength to argue with him. He hobbled over to where she was slumped, his cane taking the full weight of his frail frame with each painstaking step. She couldn't tell which creaked the loudest, the cane carrying him, or his own body. He shuffled next to her and settled down on the ground.

She could see his face clearly now, the brim of his hat no longer sufficient to hide his face. His face was a mass of wrinkles that wound around each other so tightly it looked like they might snap. It looked pinched, as if he'd been a painting and someone had grabbed his nose and pulled, the whole face ending up with a permanent squint. She couldn't quite see where the hat ended and his ears began, but before she could look too closely, the old man turned and stared at her. From that point on, all she could see were his eyes.

His eyes. They were like… like… coal. Black. Harsh. Opaque, but bristling with barely concealed fire. And they held her fast. She couldn't pull away, but then she didn't feel that she should. She didn't feel anything.

"Not every bird is an eagle, you know," he rattled.

Puddlebrain wanted to respond, but her mouth had become disconnected from the rest of her body. She could feel it hanging from her face, limp and useless as if it had been glued in place for some reason, but then that reason had been forgotten or thrown out with the old banana peels and apple cores. Her mind still ticked, but the clockwork spring had been removed.

? she thought.

"Indeed," the old man said. He was speaking quietly, but Puddlebrain realised he was only voicing part of his words. The rest were in her head. "Not every tree is an oak and not every stream you cross leads into the sea, though you'd like to think that it does."

?

"Is that the most intelligent thing I've heard you say? Methinks so." He smiled. It was a gentle smile, absent of the threat that pervaded every other aspect of him. "Not every girly is simply a girly, and not every old man is just an old man… girly."

Puddlebrain would have frowned, but her eyebrows seemed to have gone to sleep. She wondered if he knew what he was talking about. He wasn't making much sense to her, that was for sure, but that didn't mean he wasn't making any sense to himself. She'd heard Gemini, on many an occasion, waffling on about nothing and everything in a serious of conjoined sentences that had no relation to each other whatsoever. But she was a whippersnip short of a floret, so had an excuse. As far as the witch could tell, he might talk nonsense, but he did so with at least the impression of sanity.

The old man, or whatever he might be, watched her as she digested his words. He knew she was easily the apple that made the crumble in her family so she'd get it in the end. His gaze felt warm to Puddlebrain. It was soothing somehow and she was feeling less frustrated with herself. She wondered who he was. Obviously he wasn't simply an old man, just as she wasn't simply a girl. She understood that much. But for him to be here, in the centre of the Grimace, unperturbed by the menace of the forest? And then there was his reaction to her magic – it was less than an irritation to him. What sort of creature could withstand magic? She didn't know and, try as she might, she just couldn't think. Unless...

The old man broke his gaze. He was grinning broadly.

"There you go, me girly! I *knew* you could do it!"

"But..." Puddlebrain began.

She'd had an inkling of an idea for a second there. A stroke of a thought had brushed the back of her mind with a tantalising tickle, but it was snatched back as he broke the connection between them. She mentally grasped at it, but it was gone. His voice had broken the spell. But there was *something*...

"Something indeedy. Now. What would you like to ask, girly?"

"I'd like to ask you not to call me girly for one thing," she sighed. "If I stop thinking of you as just an old man."

"Of course, girly! Of course! It's a deal! Anything else?"

"Who are you?"

Turning to face the witch, his smile broadened.

"You want to know about little old me?"

His body creaked as he moved, but his movements seemed to be more fluid than they should have been. Then Puddlebrain looked down. The earth was moving beneath him. It was shifting around, helping him turn. The crumbs of mud looked like hundreds of spiders as they skittered around in a circle, taking his body with them.

"Well, of course it is, girly!" he laughed.

She noticed that the rattle was less noticeable in his cackle. It was less of an itch in her head.

"Just getting used to being like this, is all," he said. "Takes a wee bit of time and a whole lot of effort is all." He leaned forward, once again looking into her eyes. Once again, she was enraptured. "The ground, like the rain, is my friend. Thought they were yours too!"

"But…" she began again.

She was going to say that the rain *was* her friend. She was going to say the grass and the birds and the sky and all of it were her friends. But being trapped in the Grimace had seriously dented her resolve on pretty much everything. She just wasn't sure anymore. Were they her friends? Or did they just do as she wished because she was a witch? But she'd lost her powers! She hadn't been a witch for decades!

Oh, hold on. She hadn't lost her magic. She and her sisters had just… mislaid it… So the grass *could* have grown *because* she was a witch. The rain *could* have missed her *because* she was a witch. The birds *could* have spoken to her *just because she was a witch!*

She held her head in her hands. She just didn't know. And what if that was the case? What if it was all *just because*? She didn't want that! That would mean, apart from her sisters, she had nobody! The geese, who stopped by on their way to easier pickings during the winter months, only stayed for a while because they had to? Was that it? The grass in their garden only grew to a forest or shrank to a whisker on the soles or her feet because it felt forced? *Was that it?* Was she alone? Was her world a lie?

The old man put his arm around her. It felt hard and bony, but it was still something of a comfort.

"Is that what you believe?" he asked.

His voice was soft. The crackle had gone. He no longer sounded like his voice could break in two. Puddlebrain lifted her head.

"What?"

"Is that what you believe? That you're all alone? That you're nothing? An insignificant speck on the eyeball of life? A useless piece of…"

"OKOKOK!" Puddlebrain cried. "I get the point! So maybe I do! Maybe I do think that I'm just a tired old excuse for a witch. I was never the good one anyway. I was always the baby. I was always the one pushed back. So yes! Maybe I am just a big fat nothing and all my friends were fake and all my life is a lie!"

She was shaking, a stomach-wrenching mixture of anger, frustration and fear. She was ranting, she knew. She didn't know if any of it was true or if all of it was a facade. She couldn't *focus!*

"Ah yes, focus!" crooned the old man. "Focus, focus, hocus pocus! Focus is our way of saying PishPosh to the darkness and Hey-ho Daddyo to our good ol' friend normality! Focus lets us drag all our eggs into one basket, lest any of them crack. Now, girly. Have you cracked? Are you the egg, or are you the basket?"

Basketcase, more like, thought Puddlebrain, and she wasn't referring to herself.

"That's as maybe, daisy, but we've got ourselves a dilemma here, ain't we just. A dilemma of a conundrum, if you ask me, which I know you won't, but if you did, well then, we'd all be happy, wouldn't we?"

"Erm…" said Puddlebrain. Well, is was better than '?.' She shook her head. "Who are you?"

Chapter Thirty Two

"Now we get somewhere. If you'd just asked in the first, place, instead of gibber-jabbering, you could have been on your merry way, and I could go back to sleep. But oh, no. Not you, girly. Get yourself all worked up and thinking you're no good for nothing. Well, if that's what you'd be thinking, that's what you'd be doing. Just ask a straight question and you'd get a straight…"

"*WHO ARE YOU?*" Puddlebrain shouted. Oh, would he just get *on* with it? She thought. Get on with it or get *lost!*

"Get lost?" the old man smirked. "Methinks it's you who's lost. Now, seeing as you asked so nicely, I may even tell you."

He stood up, his movements no longer awkward, his joints no longer creaking. Even though he looked so old, he was more fluid than even the witch.

"I, my Lady, " he said bowing low, "am Thistle."

He straightened and looked at Puddlebrain, acting as if that one sentence explained everything.

"Thistle?"

"Thistle, indeed."

?

"And I thought we were making such progress, girly."

Puddlebrain sighed. What was the point?

"The point is what you, my girly, are going to be poked with if you don't drag you back to yourself and stop withering about!" He leaned in close. "The point," he whispered, "is that you need to get along, and quickly."

"But I don't know what to do!" Puddlebrain said.

She winced at the whiney tone in her voice. It was so unlike her to be down trodden, even when her older sisters were playing their older sister parts.

Come on girl, she told herself. *Get a grip!*

"Excellent advice!" Thistle said, suddenly prancing around her, his feet skittering across the ground, his cane lying discarded.

"Who are you, really?" Puddlebrain asked. It seemed like the most important question in the world at that moment. The location of her sisters and the townsfolk was suddenly secondary to knowing the true identity of this strange little man.

"So I'm little now, am I? And there's you a mighty redwood! Oh yes indeedy."

He danced away, snatching up his cane and flinging it high into the branches of the great oaks. Puddlebrain flinched, half expecting it to land on her head, but after a moment realized the cane wasn't coming back down. She looked upwards cautiously. The staff had vanished.

"Not vanished, girly, just returned."

Returned? The whisper of a thought that had brushed her mind resurfaced, a vague shadow like a painting seen through a net curtain. Puddlebrain deliberately ignored it, knowing that if she tried to run after it, the thought would be , playing a game of chase she would never win. She, instead, concentrated on trying to see where Thistle's hat ended and his head began. She couldn't see a gap, or even a line between the two. It was as if the hat was part of the old man's head.

Part of his head…

The cane was… returned?

And…

Puddlebrain's eyes opened wide as realization dawned. How could anyone walk amongst the Grimace if the forest didn't want them to? Why were Thistle's movements so awkward to begin with, yet now he appeared as if he could be a dancer? Was it…?

"Oh, well done! Give the girly a medal! A big shiny gold star! A trophy with her name on it! A…"

"OK!" Puddlebrain snapped. If she was correct, and Thistle's reaction hinted that she was, then perhaps he might actually be able to help her!

Thistle shut up. His eyes were twinkling, stars shining in the coal black night sky, and the sides of his mouth were raised in a barely controlled smirk.

"I knew you had it in you!" he grinned. "You just needed a nudge."

"So," Puddlebrain ventured, "*you're* the Grimace?"

It sounded crazy saying it out loud. How could this old man, who seemed to be becoming younger by the minute, be part of the forest?

"Not so daft as you might think," Thistle beamed. He pirouetted over to her side and dropped down beside her. "Not daft at all, no sir-even-though-you're-not-a-sir!"

Puddlebrain waited for something more, but he was simply grinning at her inanely.

"Well?" she asked. "Are you?"

"Yes and no," he said. "Quite and not quite. It sort of depends on who you ask and what answer they give, you see?"

Puddlebrain obviously did not see, but she decided she might as well work this through. Thistle would only tell her what he wanted to, and in his own time. She really had no place to go right at that moment so had little choice other than to wait.

"Choices, choices. You have no choice but to have a choice!" Thistle said. His head bobbed from side to side as he talked and his Puddlebrain noticed his fingers kept drumming against the ground. It was as if he was finding it difficult to keep still, or perhaps movement was new to him and he was keen to keep trying it out.

"See," he said, "you're not as dense as a midnight mist, are you? You *do* have an inkling of an idea now and again!"

Puddlebrain nodded slowly. Maybe she was right. If he were the Grimace, or at least some part of it, then he would probably spend decades immobile. He could be rooted like a tree, the wind providing his only escape. Perhaps that explained why he was so creaky to begin with and so fluid now. He had to get used to being able to walk and move about. And he wanted to take advantage of his time, hence the fidgeting.

"Indeed," said Thistle thoughtfully. His face was downcast and there was a hint of something like regret in his voice, but then it was gone and he looked up again, the beaming smile returned.

"So, you're the Grimace?" Puddlebrain asked.

She was tired of repeating herself, but it appeared to be the only way of gleaning any information. She didn't have the time to keep saying the same thing over and over again, but Thistle apparently found it difficult to answer a question before the twenty or thirtieth time of asking.

"You just need to ask the right question the right way," he said. "And then you'll get your answers. It's not so hard, you know. The same question can be asked a hundred different ways, using the same words, but if you ask it the wrong way, you'll get the wrong answer."

"Or no answer," responded Puddlebrain.

"No answer isn't the right answer, so it still counts as the wrong answer."

Well… Puddlebrain couldn't disagree with that. She needed, though, to figure out a way to ask the right answer in the right way to get the right question! Or something like that! All this digression was wasting valuable time. She was beginning to feel desperate.

Thistle reached up and cradled the witch's chin in his hand. His touch was warm and soft, almost relaxing.

"Time, "he said, his voice as gentle as his fingers, "is something we don't have to worry about."

Chapter Thirty Three

Puddlebrain frowned. Not worry? She could do nothing *but* worry! Little Whimsy was deserted! Her sisters were gone! She was lost in the Grimace and she was running vocal circles in the maze of the old man's words! How could she not worry?

Thistle giggled. "I like that," he laughed. "Vocal circles! Very good! Maze of my words! Priceless!"

Puddlebrain threw up her hands. This was pointless. She was getting nowhere. There was no option but to find her way out of the Grimace and try and find her sisters. She put her hands on the ground to push herself up. She suddenly felt spiders crawling across them and went to snatch her hands back…

… but she couldn't! Staring down, she saw why. It wasn't spiders on her hands. It was mud! The ground was still moving, just as it had beneath Thistle, but this time it had shifted over her hands, trapping them! She couldn't move! She glared at the him.

"What are you doing? Let me go!"

"I'm not doing a single little thing, girly," he smiled. "If you want to go, then go! If you don't want the help of a silly, senile old man, then be off with you." He stood up and looked down at her. "It was, I must admit, a joy to meet you. You tootle off and perhaps I'll see you again one day."

Puddlebrain could only stare helplessly as Thistle walked over to one of the oaks and placed his hand flat against its bark. He smiled at her, then pushed, and walked *into* the tree! In a second he was gone. The air of hollowness that fell on the clearing stunned the witch. It was as if all the life had been sucked from the area and she was the only thing that had been left. Her eyes were fixed on where he had been a moment before then, with a whoosh, she felt the air moving and heard the leaves rustling. She tried desperately to pull her hands free of the ground, but they were stuck fast and her struggles only seemed to make the earth grip her tighter. She was frantic and tears were streaming down her cheeks.

"Come back!" she cried. "Please!"

She froze as a chuckle sounded behind her. Twisting her body as best she could, Puddlebrain strained to see the source.

"Just my little joke," said Thistle, stepping away from the trunk of a second great oak.

"Joke?" cried Puddlebrain helplessly. "Joke? Where's the humour in this? Please tell me which part is actually funny!"

"Why, girly, all of it is!" said Thistle, dancing a little jig. He clapped his hands and chuckled. "You just need to see past it and you'll be rolling around fit to burst your belly."

Puddlebrain could feel her face flushing with anger. She was fit to burst, all right. It wasn't with the non-existent hilarity, however. Enough was beyond enough now. She'd come to the Grimace to find out... well, whatever was happening. All she had managed to do was be delayed by the Grimace itself. It had trapped her and talked her head into a spin. Maybe that was the plan all along. The forest was obviously where she'd look for her family and the rest of the villagers. Now it had her too. What if the Grimace was the one that had stolen everyone? They hadn't just been brought here, the Grimace had taken them!

She didn't notice Thistle standing in front of her until he was, suddenly, bent close, almost nose to nose. She could see the grain of his skin now. Tiny little knots like pimples on wood. Breath that smelled like fresh cut shavings.

Her thoughts froze in her mind as if a hand had wrapped itself around her brain and squeezed the juice into a cup for a drink. Being so elusive was thirsty work.

"Listen, girly," Thistle whispered.

His voice was hushed but Puddlebrain was sure she'd be able to hear it from the kitchen of her own house even with Edna's stew bubbling away. The sound wouldn't have dared fade until it reached exactly the ears it was intended for and delivered its message.

"Tell me, please, what I would be doing with a whole village full of people. They're not water or sun, so they can't feed me. They just talk and complain and they're so impatient. And they are gone so fast I would barely notice they were here at all."

Puddlebrain wondered if he was telling the truth. The Grimace could be lying. It could be (and was) confusing her to keep her there.

"If I wanted you to stay, you wouldn't be leaving" said Thistle standing, his movements so fluid you couldn't be sure he'd moved at all, if it wasn't for the fact he was no longer crouched right in front of you. "And we would not be having this fun little chat. You would be held by my branches and wouldn't be able to move for the rest of your short little life. Even a life as long as yours is a shiver of a heartbeat to me."

Puddlebrain noticed his jovial nonsense was absent, to be replaced by a much sterner and firmer manner. While he had spun her like a top previously, she preferred that to the bubbling, troubling severity that now threatened her.

"You feel threatened, girly?"

"No," she said, defiantly.

Yes, she thought, honestly.

"Don't be." Thistle's voice was suddenly softer. The hard bark had been smoothed down. "You wanted help. I find it difficult not to play games. It's so long between talking to your kind, or at all, that I forget myself and get carried away. And it takes a little of your time for me to adjust."

Puddlebrain could understand that. No-one dared enter the Grimace, so the chances to chat were few and far between.

"Your father was the last, and the only one for a long time."

Puddlebrain gasped. Her father?

"Yes. He was like you. He *felt* nature. The grass. The birds. The weather, even. That's how he knew we were in pain."

The Grimace was in pain? Did trees even feel pain?

"Not in the way you do, but we know what pain is. Your father felt it too and came to help."

Her father?

"Yes, girly. Your *father*. Stop that. Your brain is hitting thoughts of your father like a bull at a brick wall. Climb the wall. Don't be running at it with your eyes closed."

Puddlebrain coughed and shook her head, trying to make the wall topple so she could get around it. She'd spent so long being the baby of the family she wasn't particularly athletic, physically or mentally.

"Don't be putting yourself down, girly. Too many others will do that for you. Let them waste their energy and you put yours to better use."

"What did my father do?" she asked.

"We were slumbering. We do that. It passes your time until we get to ours. And a… blight… invaded us. A shadow we could not keep out. It wanted our heart and almost stole it away."

"Your heart?"

"What makes us. What gives us… this Thistle. It wanted to claim it. We almost lost ourselves."

Chapter Thirty Four

There was no longer a 'me' or an 'I' in the little man's words. It was only 'we' as if not just the Grimace as a whole, but each individual tree was talking to her.

"And my father?"

"Your father felt our pain. We don't know how. Through the rain, perhaps. Or the setting of the sun. He came and he healed us. The scars still leave their marks but your father made us… as whole as he could."

Puddlebrain wiped a tear which had sneaked out of the corner of her eye and was trailing down her cheek. Her father. She felt a swelling of emotion in her chest, but pushed it back down for fear of it forcing more tears out.

Thistle watched her for a moment, letting her feel the rush of pride, love and loss. The Grimace was private. It preferred to keep itself in and others out and had remained constant for so long even it couldn't remember its own origins. It spent great lengths of time in solitude, speaking only with the wind and the rain and so was unaccustomed to people and their impatience.

Sometimes, though, necessity came a-knocking and the Grimace had to heed the call. This girl's father had helped stay the shadow's touch, and now that strength and power had been passed to his youngest daughter. If the shadow was walking again, then only she would be able to stop it. If she couldn't, then the Grimace may, again, be unable to fight it and its heart would be taken.

The Grimace was eternal. Its roots spread so far beneath the earth that it had become a part of almost every town and village, even though they didn't realise it. All trees, from sapling to great oak to weeping willow were children of the Grimace. The apple tree in the garden of the Fudge's of Armitage Avenue, Whipenstair. The elm with the tree-house in the park, way over at the back of Deringer Town. The odd little growth, a mass of twigs somehow managing to stick together in a birds' nest of branches that grew behind the school in Little Whimsy itself.

But here, in its densest, darkest centre, you could feel the Grimace's breath. You could sense that it lived. If you ever dared to enter, that was, and if it ever saw fit to allow you.

Puddlebrain, in actual real-life fact, was *speaking* to the Grimace, and it was *responding!* And wrapping her up in riddles, too, much like the bandages that Fiddle McFilip had been swathed in the time he'd fallen off his roof.

Well, he *had* been trying to fix some loose tiles in the pouring rain. It didn't help that he wore glasses so couldn't see where he was going because of the rain streaked lenses. He'd been in hospital for over a month and always preferred to walk backwards after that, using a mirror to see where he was going. He blamed it on an awkward twist of his hip from the fall. Others just thought it was because of the knock on his head.

But now, she had to go. She had to return and fight this shadow. Find her sisters and the rest of the villagers. Did they deserve it? They'd been happy to blame the witches and roast them like turkeys. Surely it would be better – and quieter – for Puddlebrain and her siblings to leave the villagers right where they were.

No. She couldn't do that. Edna might have done. She was the oldest of the three and had a hint of spite running down her spine that popped up every now and again to cause a little havoc. Gemini would quite possibly have just wondered when the stew was going to be ready, oblivious to anything other than the rumbling in her tumbling (as she liked to call it) and the hour's proximity to thirteen o'clock. Puddlebrain was sometimes, she thought, far too nice. She had to help them. She just couldn't help herself.

With a hefty sigh which fell out of her and plopped onto the ground, the newly-witchly-witch stood. She looked at Thistle for a moment and he stood watching her back.

"I should go," she said, finally.

"Well said," the little man replied. "Indeed you should. Time is wasting away, even for us."

Puddlebrain looked around. She had no idea which way she had entered this clearing and, equally, no idea how to get out again. She could just pick a direction and hope it would be the right one - and hope that the Grimace would clear a path for her - or she could close her eyes and see which way her feet took her.

"The way you came is the way you leave," said Thistle.

She turned to ask what this latest riddle might mean but he was nowhere to be seen. His words hung in the air like a mist on a chill autumn morning, clinging to nothing and drifting on a sigh.

Well, that was certainly her cue to leave.

Chapter Thirty Five

"Come on feet," she said, looking down. "Show me the way."

Puddlebrain, not actually expecting her feet to guide her without her guiding them, simply walked forward. As she neared the wall of trees, they parted, branches creaking and moving to create a tunnel of wood and leaf. She had no choice, she knew, but to follow it and hope Thistle – and the Grimace – would lead her out. She was wary, wondering if the forest would actually lead her in circles, an eternity spent wandering around with no hope of escape.

It was a chance she had to take, for the villagers, her sisters and herself. For so long she'd been in their shade. Edna and Gemini treated her as if she was the baby and the rest of Little Whimsy followed suit. Now she had to prove she wasn't. Hopefully then she might believe herself it too.

She walked a few paces into the tunnel before looking back. The trees had closed behind her, cutting off any hope of escape, should she have wanted one. Escape, however, was not an option. What would she do? Where could she go? No, Puddlebrain had one goal and that was to save all those who had, in one form or another, mistreated or looked down upon her. Without wondering why she might do such a thing for those who, quite possibly, would have to think twice, thrice or never even imagine doing the same for her, she continued on.

As she walked, the branches, trunks and roots ahead moved in a fluid, snake-like motion. The creaking was gone and, instead, the trees almost hissed into place, creating a confined but clear path for her to follow. She tried, a couple of times, to sprint, hoping to outrun The Grimace and choose her own way through to the outside world but the forest was too fast for her. The passageway slithered together in anticipation of her dash and kept her exactly where it wanted her to be.

She wanted to vent, to cry out at her frustration of being led rather than simply being able to just *go*, but knew it would be pointless - and knew, without the guidance, this witch would quite possibly never been seen again.

With a sigh of acceptance, she carried on walking. Considering it was night-time, Puddlebrain discovered she could see quite well. There seemed to be no light seeping in through the branches from the star-filled sky, nor were the trees glowing in any way that the witch could perceive. Still, she could see when she expected to be fumbling around. Perhaps her eyes had adjusted to the dark as if she'd enjoyed a diet of carrots for the past century. You never saw a blind rabbit. Maybe the Grimace was shining in a way she couldn't tell. Either way, Puddlebrain was pleased she didn't have to feel her way along the tunnel. She could easily have tripped, broken a limb and been stranded.

Suddenly, the path opened up. It wasn't exactly a clearing such as the one she'd met Thistle in, being covered over and enclosed. It was more like a room. Perhaps the cellar back at the house. Either way, something was before her that made the breath catch in her throat on its way out to the big wide world. She stopped dead in her tracks, her feet matching her breath for its inability to move.

Billy!

Growing out of the ground, roots spreading and twisting with those of the rest of the Grimace, was the gnome. In the short time the pair had been parted, moss had already taken hold and was covering the lower part of his face in a dark green and yellow beard. Cobwebs spun across the large boles that made up his ears and, in one, a spider with long, spindly legs three times the length of his yellow and black striped body dined on a beetle of some sort.

The spider skittered away as the witch ran forward. She hugged him close, ignoring the hardness of his skin and how it grazed her cheek. Tears ran from her closed eyes and trickled from cheek to bark where it soaked into the wood. How could she do this to her friend? How could she abandon him?

A sob escaped her mouth.

"Quit yer whining!" said a voice. Small hands were pushing at her body. "And gerroff me!"

Puddlebrain tumbled backwards, confused.

Thistle?

No!

BILLY!

She threw herself forward again, her arms wrapping around the gnome tightly. Billy grunted and tried vainly to push her away again. Unsuccessful, he gave up and let her hold him.

After a few moments that seemed to linger about each other just to see how far they could drag time he had to try again.

"You're... strangling... me...! Can't... breath...!"

"Oh!" exclaimed Puddlebrain, letting go. "I'm sorry! I didn't mean... I mean... I wanted to..."

"Yeah, yeah. I know. You wanted to say how sorry you were for turning me all woody-like and leaving me behind. You wanted to beg for my forgiveness and promise to do my bidding for the rest of your life. I know, I know."

Puddlebrain blinked.

"Erm... no. Not quite," she said. "I was pleased to see you again."

"Oh well," said Billy. "It was worth a try."

"I mean, I am sorry, truly, but..."

"Forget it. It was quite nice being a tree for a bit. Gives you time to think when you can't move. You have to entertain yourself with your thoughts."

"What did you think about?"

"I thought about how I'd like to turn you into a tree and wondered how you'd like it if spiders were crawling around in your ears!"

Billy shook his head and wiggled his fingers in his ears.

"Just in case you wondered, it wasn't quite nice at all. It was decidedly *not* nice. So thanks *very* much!"

Puddlebrain looked down. "I'm s..."

"Sorry, sorry, sorry. I know. I get it. Forget it. I'm not barking mad now, so just forget it."

"Barking mad?"

"Blimey, witch! Don't you recognise a joke when it slaps you in the face?"

Puddlebrain did know what a joke was, but wasn't used to being slapped in the face by one. She shook her head, not knowing what to say. She'd missed her friend's sarcasm filled comments, as insulting as they often were. The witch told herself she would do her very best not to turn him into anything at all from that point on, even if she felt he really deserved it. The remarks were just his way. She could deal with that.

At least she hoped she could. Still, this wasn't the time for joking. They had things to do, somehow. They had people to save – again, somehow. They had to move.

This brought to light another problem. Billy had been a tree, roots, knots and all. Was he still rooted to the ground, his toes digging into the mud to spread like a spider's web of wood?

"Can you move?" she asked, nervously.

"I can move a lot faster than you, even with these twigs still sticking out of my feet!"

Puddlebrain looked down and Billy wiggled his toes. Tiny pieces of wood, each with a leaf attached, poked from the gaps between them.

"Oh..."

"Is that the best you can do? 'Oh'?"

Puddlebrain scratched her head. She hadn't expected that.

"I didn't expect that," she said. "I'm still getting used to being able to do magic stuff again."

She paused, not daring to look at the gnome in the face.

"Maybe it'll wear off after a bit?"

"Wear off? You really should read a handbook on finger twirling or whatever it is you do. Preferably before you do any of it anymore!"

Puddlebrain was eager to get going, but she was unsure how to broach the subject with her friend.

"Come on," sighed the gnome. "We can't stick around here. We need to get a shift on."

Puddlebrain laughed nervously.

"What you laughing at?" snorted Billy.

"You made a joke! 'Stick around'!"

Billy stared.

"Clearly you *don't* know a joke," he said quietly.

"Oh," said Puddlebrain.

Billy poked her.

"Got you," he said.

He turned and ran off towards a wall of branches which opened up into a new tunnel. He stopped at the entrance and looked back.

"Unless you want me to leaf you here, I suggest you drag your backside into gear and come on!"

Puddlebrain blinked, smirked and ran after her friend.

As they left, the branches behind them twisted and intertwined. Thistle stepped forward into the clearing.

"Good luck," he whispered as the path closed behind them.

Chapter Thirty Six

With no way of knowing in which direction they were going, the witch and the gnome could only follow the tunnel created by the unfolding branches of the Grimace. Only a few bends broke the continuous line the trees created, the pair had no choice but to go forward and keep moving. The path closed swiftly behind them, forcing them to keep their speed up lest they be impaled upon the twigs which poked out from the wall of trees.

"How far do you think we are from the outside?" panted Puddlebrain.

"It won't matter with those trees chasing us!" replied Billy, his breath a rasping rattle. "If they don't slow down, I'm going to have to make them before they catch us!"

A root sprang up from the ground, tripping him up and sending him sprawling. Puddlebrain paused long enough to help him up and for him to shake off her hands with a grunt and they were running again.

"That told you," she said, her breathlessness disguising the laughter in her voice.

Billy opened his mouth to say something but suddenly there was no more forest.

The trees ended and there was an abrupt feeling of being ejected. He stopped dead and Puddlebrain only managed to avoid running into him by twisting to the side and tumbling to the ground. She landed roughly, her head slamming against the earth. Billy stared, not quite able to understand either his friend's predicament or the absence of the forest. When Puddlebrain didn't move, his senses whirled around from their scattering and returned to his mind. He blinked and shook his head, then knelt quickly beside the witch.

"Don't you go sleeping now," he hissed, not daring to touch her.

Puddlebrain didn't move. Billy reached out, his hand hovering above her. If he laid a finger on her, he was sure she would break. She was just a girl. A girl who could spin a spell, but just a girl. He had spent so long worrying about and protecting her. He watched as she took on the weight of her sisters' resentment and frustration at the loss of their powers. They thought him brusque, he knew. Obnoxious, probably. Many times, he thought they were merely tolerating his presence rather than welcoming him. But he was a gnome. That's how everyone treated him, including other gnomes. It didn't mean he didn't care. Quite the contrary, in fact. The more annoying or biting he was, the more he felt. He was a gnome. Feelings were an itch they couldn't scratch and, as such, they buried them under bandages of annoyance and biting comments.

"Move your noggin," he told her. "You'd better not have broken that ground. It won't take kindly if you've stained that grass with your blood."

Puddlebrain groaned and Billy almost hugged her. It took an effort for him not to throw his arms around her in relief.

"About time," he told her. "No sleeping on the job."

She opened her eyes and looked at him, blinking to clear the blurriness that fuzzed his figure.

"You shouldn't be so boring then," she said quietly.

"Can you stand?"

"Can you?" she asked. "Oh, you already are."

"Oooh, so says the super tall little girl who's laid out as if the sun's going to shine tomorrow and she's just waiting to do top up her tan."

Puddlebrain snorted. It was a combination of laughter and the pain the humour was inflicting on her throbbing head. She pushed herself up, standing unsteadily on legs that felt as if they thought they were still laying down. Billy offered a hand but she didn't accept it.

"I've been around you too long," she said. "I can do this myself."

"At least I've taught you something."

She nodded then instantly regretted it as a wave of nausea threatened to empty the contents of her stomach all over the gnome.

"We need to go," Billy pointed out.

"Then let's do just that."

"Where are we going now? The village?"

It wasn't like Billy to be undecided, or to at least show it. Indecision was a weakness his kind couldn't indulge in. They were easy pickings for other, more focussed, gnomes who would happily take advantage of you if you were prone to the odd pause before choosing which path to take.

Puddlebrain, despite feeling as if she needed to lie down for at least a week, had already made the choice. She pointed.

"There."

Chapter Thirty Seven

The Hole had been oblivious to the pair standing only a short distance away from its maw. At the sudden attention, it perked up. It had remained hidden, forgotten and dorment for so long, apart from the grumbling in its depths, it didn't know how to react. It smiled, as much as a hole can, anyway. In actual fact, holes can't smile. Their shape doesn't change unless affected by the elements or a big spade. This hole, *the* Hole, was different however. It began to glow.

Puddlebrain scratched her ear.

"Fleas?" asked Billy.

"What?"

"Every so often, you scratch our ear. Either you have an itch that keeps sneaking back, or you have an infestation." He shuddered. "A steam bath is known to help."

"I…"

Puddlebrain looked at her hand as if seeing it for the first time. She turned it, wiggling the fingers.

"Oh," she said.

"Oh?"

"I do that sometimes," she said.

"I know," said Billy. "I just said so. Does it mean something?"

"Yes,"

"Well?"

"What?"

"What does it mean? You witches are the worst!"

"Erm… It means something bad is happening. Or has happened. Or is going to happen." She shrugged, not realising she'd even been doing it.

"Well," sighed Billy, "that's comforting. At least you're specific in your madness."

The Hole, wondering how its luminosity was going unnoticed, gritted its non-existent teeth and squeezed a little more light up from its depths. Puddlebrain's finger was still pointing in its direction but they were too engrossed in their conversation to look that way.

"Fine," said the gnome. "Let's g..."

Now he looked. *Now* he saw the glow.

"It looks like you were right," he said.

"It had to happen sooner or later," said the witch.

Billy didn't notice her comment, or he would have leapt on the opening it gave him to make a perfectly sarcastic retort and ridden it all the way home. He approached the Hole carefully.

"Billy," whispered Puddlebrain. "Wait."

He ignored her. The light was warm. It was inviting. It made him want to touch it and climb down into its cocoon. Her sudden hand on his shoulder snapped him from his daze.

"What are you doing?" she asked.

"I..." Billy looked confused. He shook his head, blinking. "I'm going down that there hole, obviously," he said. "That's where you said, so that's what I'm doing. You joining me or not?"

Puddlebrain frowned but didn't say anything more. She simply nodded, wondering what it was about the strange light from the Hole that had so entranced her friend.

"Is that you?" he asked.

"Is what me?"

"That shimmering. The humming. Is it you?"

"I can't hear any humming and the light is steady."

"My ears are bigger than yours. My eyes too. Trust me – it's unsteady and it's humming."

Puddlebrain squinted to see if she could see any disturbance in the glow but it appeared to be at a constant brightness. She tilted her head to try and let any other noises slip into her ear, but all she could hear were their footsteps on the grass.

"It's not me," she said.

"Didn't think so," said Billy. "Too pretty."

They arrived at the lip of the Hole and looked down, the witch carefully lest she fell in and the gnome brazenly, seemingly not caring either way. He appeared to be shrugging on a coat of bravado to conceal his momentary lapse a moment ago, wrapping it about himself tightly so none of his uncertainty could leak out.

"Let's go," he said gruffly.

"How are we going to get down?" asked Puddlebrain.

It looked a long way down and, though it had faded somewhat from the general population's memory, she did recall it supposedly going on forever with a bottom that forgot to bottom. She told Billy this.

"What?"

"It's meant to be *bottomless*."

"Nothing is bottomless!" he sneered. "Except, maybe, your dunsicity."

"Dunsicity?"

"You're being a dunce. Dunsicity."

"There's no such word."

"There is now!" he snapped. "But stop being irrelevant. We'd best start climbing. We may be here a long time if, indeed, its bottom doesn't exist. A bit like your sense."

"Wait," she said.

She was a witch. It was about time she was witchy.

She raised the finger she had just pointed and pointed again, this time at the walls of the Hole. She flicked it a little and muttered under her breath. There was a low creaking sound and they felt a slight tremor beneath their feet. Something started to push through the ground beside them, looking like the spindly legs of an abnormally large spider. Billy winced and raised his foot, intending on bringing it down hard on the arachnid, but Puddlebrain stopped him.

"Wait," she said again.

Billy waited, keeping his foot lifted. He wobbled slightly but was unwilling to set down his weapon. Not that a gnome's foot could do much damage to something that seemed to keep on growing, but he'd do his best. Finally, the creature broke ground fully and revealed itself. It was neither a spider nor, really, a creature of any sort. Billy lowered his foot slowly.

"How is that going to help?" he asked, bemused.

"They."

Before questions could be asked the *thing* began to answer them by shaking violently. The creaking became a sharp tearing and a line appeared on its back. The line opened up into a rip that split it in two. When they separated, the shaking stopped. What remained was a pair of large, ten legged, wooden beetles.

"Climb on," said Puddlebrain.

"After you."

"There's no need to be scared," Puddlebrain smiled, though fear was certainly creeping up along her back, tickling it humourlessly. Whatever was waiting for them had stolen the villagers. It had taken her sisters. She needed to take them back. Fear was a joke with no punchline.

"Who's afraid? Not me!" Billy growled. "Gnomes don't know fear. Don't be passing yours on to me because it won't work."

"Of course not. I wouldn't dream of it."

"Why, exactly, do we need to go down there?"

Puddlebrain shrugged. Where else was there? She assumed the Grimace had led them there deliberately and hadn't just ejected them randomly. Besides, there was a light coming from its depths. That wasn't normal and, as such, bore investigation.

"Because," she said.

"Fair enough. Ladies first," Billy said. "Or, in their absence, you."

Puddlebrain poked him, smiling. The dry humour was their best defence and if they needed to hold it up like a shield, they'd die smiling.

Die.

Perhaps not the best word to use.

"Watch where you're shoving that finger," said Billy. "It's loaded."

Puddlebrain turned to the spider-like mass of roots she'd summoned and climbed onto its back. One of the legs reached around to hold her in place.

"Let's go for a ride," she said.

Billy shook his head but followed suit. Once they were both in place and secure, their mounts moved to the edge and began to climb in and down.

"What do you call these things?" he asked.

"Whatever they want to be called. I'm not going to argue."

"Briders. That's what they are."

"Briders?" Puddlebrain asked in between the *oofs* and *umphs* that were being forced from her with each lunging movement.

"Branches and spiders. Briders." Billy smiled, proud of himself and wearing the pride as a fake moustache to disguise his discomfort.

Puddlebrain didn't answer. She was holding on tightly, not entirely sure the slender length of wood wrapped around her was strong enough to hold her weight. She could see the gnome was gripping just as tightly as she was and gritted her teeth. She suddenly longed for some of Edna's bladderwrack soup with a double helping of Gemini's nonsense. She found it hard to believe she might miss the way things were. Being constantly reminded that she was the youngest, even though she was probably three times as old as any of the other villagers, had been tiring. So had the bickering. She'd found, since spending time with Billy that she actually liked the sarcasm. She wanted it back. She opened her mouth to say something that might prompt a suitable response from her friend but closed it again. Billy's brow was so furrowed she was sure you could plant potatoes in there. His eyes were shut tight and his knuckles were white. She left him with his panic and hoped, by the time they'd reached the bottom he had overcome it.

She hoped she had overcome her own too.

Chapter Thirty Eight

The Briders moved steadily, matching their pace with each other to the point that they were in sync with their movements. The same legs would be inserted deep into the earth by each of them, and the same rocking motion would shake their passengers. Puddlebrain had never created life before – if, indeed, they could be called 'alive'. They seemed to be but she wasn't sure. She had wanted something, needed it, and that something had appeared. It wasn't, at all, what she had expected but it seemed to be serving its purpose. They were descending and that's what they had to do. It was better than climbing down. Or falling.

She yearned for Billy to be right. The Hole couldn't be bottomless.

Could it?

The light that had been emanating from the mouth of the Hole had been following them as they moved. She hadn't realised it at first then, when she looked up (she had yet to find the courage to look down), she found she couldn't see the opening. There was only darkness above them. She knew the glow was nothing to do with her but wasn't about to complain. If it had been absent, she felt sure they would have been suffocated by the night.

She started to count each time they moved down a foot or so, trying to gauge how far they were travelling. When she was half way to a thousand, she gave up. She looked over to Billy, concerned at his continued silence and couldn't help but laugh. He wasn't silent. He was snoring softly. Oh, the luxury of sleep!

She was about to rouse him when the Briders stopped. Puddlebrain looked down. The light spread out beneath them. They had arrived. As one, the Briders extended their rear roots, seeming to flow into them until they had moved from the walls to the floor.

"Billy," she whispered. The gnome didn't move. "*Billy!*"

"Let me sleep," he muttered.

"I think you've slept enough," she said.

Billy's eyes snapped open and he looked around, suddenly alert.

"Oh," he said.

They were in a low cave. The light hung around them like a mist, clinging but looking as if an errant breeze might blow it away any moment. The walls of the cave were smooth. Too smooth for a natural formation. Billy ran his hand over the rock, feeling for the slightest bump or crack.

"It's warm," he said.

Puddlebrain felt the wall. It did feel warm. It should have been cold. Slick with moisture. Warm and dry and smoother than the silk her mother used to spin when she was young was unnatural.

There was an opening on the far side of the cave. She started towards it.

"What if there's something down there?" Billy hissed. "Or someone?"

"That's what we're here for," she told him. "So I'm hoping there is."

"You're going to get yourself killed. Or taken. Or vanished."

"That's what I have you here for."

"Me? Now you want me around? You're not going to turn me into a twig?"

"I haven't decided yet. Stick around."

"Hilarious," growled Billy. He stormed off in front of her, pleased the light seemed to be willing to follow him. Puddlebrain hurried after. She was pleased also - that she had been able to prompt him (she preferred not to think that she'd manipulated her friend) into moving.

They entered the tunnel. The witch had to bend slightly to avoid scraping the top of her head on the rock ceiling and she kept a hand on Billy's shoulder for support. He opened his mouth to stab a jibe at her but thought better of it. The time for sarcasm had passed. It would, he hoped, come again but at that particular time, silence was the best idea. Besides, though he'd never admit it, her touch was comforting. He would worry about whether or not he was going soft later, when the sharpness of his wit could be revisited.

The tunnel seemed to be almost as long as the hole they'd come down. If they hadn't had the light, they both felt they would be unable to move at all. Bold plans and a need to save their family and fellow villagers had spurred them into action. Such problems seemed to have faded into the darkness, leaving behind distant memories blurred by an increasing sense of foreboding.

In other words, they were scared. Only their mutual contact and the Hole's glow kept them from shrinking down and becoming like the rock that surrounded them. Cold, hard and unmoving.

And then, before their thoughts could wrap around their ankles and tie them down or drag them back, the tunnel ended.

The light extinguished.

The darkness surrounded them.

And they could hear breathing. Deep, raspy and harsh as if each breath was forced to travel over razor blades to exit the mouth and, in the process, was becoming shredded.

"Is that you?" whispered Billy, wishing for the hand on his shoulder to still be the witch's.

"No, I thought it was you," she responded, hoping the shoulder beneath her hand still belonged to the gnome.

It took a second, stretched by the tension between them, for them to realise that the sound was, in fact, both of them. They were panting but trying to hold their collective breaths. Their bodies' struggle was causing them to rip the air from their lungs with each exhalation.

"Shhh," said Billy. "I thought I heard something."

"You shush," retorted Puddlebrain. "So did I!"

"We would appreciate it if you could both be quiet. We are trying to play."

The pair's ragged breathing stopped. Their heartbeats tripped over themselves in their hurry to fill in the breaks left by the halted gasps.

"That wasn't you, was it?" Puddlebrain asked.

"Nor was it you, was it?" Billy responded.

"It was *we*."

"Who… Who are you?" asked Puddlebrain, her voice hovering hesitantly on the darkness as if afraid to venture any further out.

"We are the Multitude."

Chapter Thirty Nine

Heartbeats held their breaths, slamming to a stop in the chests of the pair of intrepid explorers. Their hands found each other, hoping to gain some strength from one another. And failing.

Puddlebrain was retreating into herself, feeling just as she had when her sisters had been there and their powers hadn't. Billy, on the other hand, was becoming increasingly angry with himself. Where was his Gnomish pride? Where had his Gnomish arrogance and self-importance scampered off to? He was being dragged down by the witch's self-pity and it was affecting his judgement. He had felt his heart freeze and had been aware of his lungs being unwilling to work properly. He needed to stop this nonsense and stand up for himself.

As much as a Gnome could.

Voices from the emptiness should be afraid of *him*, not the other way around. *He* should lead the way. Take charge. He moved closer to the witch.

"Do something," he whispered.

"We would recommend not doing something," said the Multitude. It was heavy, as if it bore the weight of a hundred people speaking in one voice. "We recommend doing nothing. We recommend joining us."

"Joining you?" asked Puddlebrain. Her own voice was unsteady, quaking next to a behemoth such as that coming from the darkness.

"Just as your friends and neighbours did. Join us as your sisters did."

Puddlebrain didn't have time to react. She had no time to process what had just been said. Without thinking, she raised her hands and splayed her fingers, letting go of Billy and ignoring the sharp yelp he made. There was a flash that caused the gnome to shield his eyes and sudden light radiated from Puddlebrain's hands, filling the cavern and banishing the shadows.

In the centre of the floor, drawing spirals in the dust with her finger, was a girl.

"Hello there," said Puddlebrain. Billy lowered his arm as she snapped her fingers to release the illumination and allow it free reign to keep the darkness at bay.

The girl looked up, smiled, and returned to her doodling. She was small. Young. Her clothes were pale rags that struggled to hold themselves together. He skin was paler still and her hair was long, a dirty blonde, and looked as if it had never been brushed.

"Are you lost? Did you see who just spoke? Where are your parents?" Puddlebrain stepped forward towards the girl, but Billy laid a warning hand on her arm. He shook his head.

"Who are you?" he asked suspiciously.

The girl looked at them without speaking. Her face was blank, giving no sign that she had heard any of their questions. Billy and Puddlebrain looked at each other, frowning, then returned their gaze to the silent figure sitting on the cold stone floor. Finally, she rubbed her hand over the dust patters, erasing them. With a sigh, she pushed herself to her feet.

"We are the Multitude," she said.

"And what's that, exactly?" Billy was beginning to feel a little braver and more like his over confident self. Granted, he was speaking to a small girl, so there was no real threat.

Even so, he was uneasy and his uneasiness stopped his confidence turning to arrogance.

"We are the Multitude."

"Thank you for clearing that up," Billy sneered.

"What are you doing?" Puddlebrain whispered. "Don't antagonise her!"

"Antagonise her? Even if she's not just the girl she appears, I'm fed up with being afraid. I'm a Gnome and that *means* something!"

"What does it mean?" the girl asked.

She took a step forward, her manner bold. Puddlebrain stepped behind the her friend, instantly berating herself for the action. Billy held his ground, though he could almost feel it shaking beneath him. Or perhaps the shaking was his own body. He gulped.

"What?"

"What does it mean to be a gnome? We would like to know."

"Why do you keep saying 'we'?" he asked. "There's only you. One of you."

"We are the Multitude," the girl said. "We are all. What doesn it mean to be a gnome?"

"It means… I mean… It means…" Billy could think of nothing to say. He wasn't expecting to be asked and so had nothing prepared. He knew, inside, exactly what it meant. Being brave to the point of being foolish. Obstinate and self-important and insufferably rude. Things to be proud of. But how did he put that into words?

"You'll find out," said Puddlebrain, finally stepping forward. "I don't care – we don't care – who you are. Do you have anything to do with my sisters disappearing? And the villagers? What about them?"

"No-one has disappeared," said the Multitude. "All are here."

"Where? There's no way out of this cave except the way we came in and they're certainly not lined up waiting for breakfast," Billy said, taking strength from the witch's uneasy composure.

"They are here," said the girl, her voice thickening with each word as if an echo was coming from within her. "They are here and they will always be so."

"Talk sense," insisted Puddlebrain. "Stop speaking in riddles."

"Yes," agreed Billy. "That's my job."

"Riddles are for those who need to hide their words with trickery and deception. Like a gnome. We are the Multitude. We have no need of such things. We speak the truth."

The depth to her voice was growing. Both gnome and witch looked around to see if there were, in fact, others in the cave. They were sure they could hear more than one person speaking.

Then Puddlebrain thought of something.

"What is the Multitude?"

"We are the Multitude," said the girl.

"Yes, we know that. But what are you?"

"We are the shadows. We are the light. We are everyone and we are everything."

"Riddles!" snorted Billy. "Tell us what you've done with the villagers. Don't make us angry."

"Anger is for those who…"

"Enough with the farty-brained quotes!" snapped Billy. "Just tell us!"

"We have. *We* are the Multitude. We are all. Join us."

"You've taken them, haven't you?" said Puddlebrain. "They're in you, somehow."

"We take no-one. They join us."

"Did you ask them?"

"Consent is not required. All join us. As will you."

"We will not!" Billy shouted. He crouched with his hands up, prepared to fight.

"Billy, wait," said Puddlebrain. "We need to get everyone out."

"I'll beat them out of her!"

"*Stop!*"

He stopped. The witch had her finger pointed at him. He could read the implied threat.

"Multitude," she said, ignoring the look of disgust on her friend's face. "Return my family to me. Return the villagers."

The girl laughed, her head thrown back and all the voices within her joining in. The sound shook the walls, causing dust and small fragments to fall. Abruptly, the laughter ceased and the girl stared at the witch.

"No."

Puddlebrain took a step back and raised her hands.

"Yes," she said quietly.

"They are with us now. They must stay with us. We are the Multitude and we are all. You will join us. You will give us energy and power."

"And what do you intend on doing with that energy and power?"

The girl twirled around, becoming the youngster she seemed to be. She danced about, kicking up the dust.

"We will consume!" she giggled, clearly having fun with the situation. "And with you joining us, we will be absolute!"

"Absolute?" Puddlebrain asked. "What is so special about us?"

"Not the gnome," said the girl, smiling. "Just you. Just the witch. Just the magic!"

She stopped dancing suddenly. Her eyes were black. Her hair was rising, as if filled with static, to create a wiry halo about her head. Her fingers became claws, the nails elongating into talons. There was a swirl at the edges of the light cast by Puddlebrain as the shadows thickened and swelled. The dark mist rolled across the floor towards the girl, entering her mouth and eyes. Her grin widened as she began to grow rapidly. Before the friends could recover from the shock change of events, the Multitude's head was almost at the roof of the cave.

"JOIN US."

Its voice was booming, rumbling through the rock to shake the bones of the pair. There was a vibrancy to it that seemed to tug as them, enticing them forward, whispering to them that there was nothing more pleasurable than being a part of the Multitude. It was *all.* It was *everything.* It was *essential.*

Billy took a step forward, unable to stop his body responding to the call.

The girl, now massive and needing to stoop as she was so large, reached forward.

"Billy!" shouted Puddlebrain.

The girl's hand opened to grab a hold of the diminutive gnome. Suddenly, he pulled something from beneath his tunic. A long, sharp length of wood. He jammed it hard into the enormous palm, twisting it as he pushed. With a scream that pierced their eardrums the way the shard had the palm, the hand was snatched back.

"*WE ARE THE MULTITUDE!*" she shouted, pulling the stake out and casting it aside. "*JOIN US OR BE CRUSHED!*"

She clenched her fist and held it above Billy's head, looking directly at Puddlebrain.

"The choice is yours, witch!"

"There is no choice," Puddlebrain answered, her jaw clenched as tightly as the fist. "*We* will never join you!"

"Then you will die."

The Multitude raised its hand higher and brought it down hard upon Billy. Puddlebrain dived forward, pushing him out of the way, but he twisted to try and avoid it smashing down on him. Puddlebrain caught him off centre and both were sent sprawling. The fist barely missed the witch but caught Billy's ankle.

There sound of splintering bone tore through the noise from the stone floor cracking and he cried out. The hand lifted and Billy vomited when he saw his ruined foot. Puddlebrain ran to him, her back to the Multitude.

"No!" she said uselessly. "I'm so sorry!"

"Don't be stupid," he said, panting through the pain. Tears welled in his eyes but his face was set, cold and determined. "Stop her."

"How?"

"You're a witch! Do your witchy things!"

Chapter Forty

"A witch who does not know her own powers," sneered the girl. "You are nothing! Join us and we will be everything!"

"NEVER!" she shouted, standing and turning to face their attacker.

"THEN DIE!"

The girl suddenly shrank down to her original size, the air being pulled from Billy and Puddlebrain's lungs to the fill the void left behind. Puddlebrain staggered but held her place. Her friend wavered, his body shaking as the lack of oxygen served to emphasise the agony shooting up from his ankle. The light seemed to shiver and dip as if it, too, was affected by the change in air pressure.

The flickering increased slightly, then pulled in towards the Multitude. It hung about her like a haze clinging to a river – not quite trapped, but not wishing to move on and leave its host.

"What's happening?" whispered Billy.

Puddlebrain didn't answer. She was entranced. Magic was at play. A dark magic. A power so much greater than her own. It was sure, where hers was untested. Strong, where hers had so long been slumbering within her slight frame. She was just the youngest sister, downtrodden by her siblings. She had yet to find her place in her own family, let alone the world. In the eyes of her family, she was the butt of their jokes. How was she meant to combat whatever this girl – this Multitude – really was?

'Do your witchy things,' Billy had said. It was all she *could* do, but first, she needed to know what she was facing.

"What are you?"

The girl looked at her.

"We… are… the… Multitude!"

Each word was spaced out evenly, spoken in a calm monotone. Each word drove home a feeling of dread. Each word was a stab in the eye of the witch.

With each word, the girl's body shook and blurred. At first, it looked as if she was moving to the side or back, but then Puddlebrain realised that wasn't the case. The Multitude was… *multiplying!*

The flickering continued, becoming a pulse of darkness in the light. As it beat a heartbeat's throb, a shadow stepped away from the girl. Another. And another. Continuing on, the cave behind her rapidly filled with murky imitations of the original.

"Meet the sisters who look down on you," she said, a sinister glee coating her words until they dripped menace. "Meet the villagers who fear you and whom you despise."

The voice didn't just come from the girl. Every one of the shadowy versions of herself spoke in unison. Rather than being deafening or echoing, the voices fell flat, devoid of emotion or substance. The words crawled towards the pair, taking on a life of their own, spidering over the stone floor.

"We are once more what we were before, when your father fought to vanquish us. We are what we were before the Grimace stood against us. Yes we are more now. We are all."

"My father? What do you know of my father?"

"We know you are a shadow of him."

"WHAT DO YOU WANT?" Puddlebrain shouted, her fear forgotten, trampled by the anger that was building inside of her. How dare this creature speak of her sisters like that? She knew exactly how she was treated in her home! But it was *her* home! *Her* sisters! *Her* life! And her father? He was her memory alone!

"YOU!"

The shadow entities swarmed together around the girl, morphing into a solid body of black that started to soak up the witch's light. It lunged forward at Puddlebrain, a hundred dusky tentacles stretching out, the night reaching for her.

There was a deep screech of agony and Puddlebrain was pushed back by a pain wracked gnome. Billy, his weight fully on his wrecked ankle, threw himself in the path of the Multitude's onslaught. He vanished into the veil of darkness, his screams drowning in the sea of nothing that engulfed him.

Puddlebrain landed sharply, pain jabbing at her back from the hard floor. She lay still for a second, stunned, then scrambled to her feet.

"NOOOO!"

Thought was something she could not afford. Fear, of the Multitude or of her own abilities, had to be put aside. Her sisters were possibly lost or perhaps trapped inside the creature. She would deal with that soon. She had only one objective. Only a single fixation.

The malicious cloud attacking her friend.

She raised her hands and spread her fingers. She searched for the spell she needed to bring forth her magic. She needed something. Instinct had escaped her and she had to entice it with a spoken word.

The shadows retreated, dropping the limp body of Billy. As Puddlebrain watched, he lifted up and… dissolved. He dissolved! His body faded, turning to smoke, and joined the mass that was swirling around the girl.

A girl who now advanced on the witch.

Puddlebrain could have stepped back. She might have run. She did neither.

She knew the word. A name.

"Billy."

She brought her hands together, clapping them loudly. Light, brighter than that which had filled the cave and been diminished by the Multitude, exploded from between her fingers. It surged outwards, a blinding radiance that wrapped around the witch with a whirlpool of luminosity.

The Multitude reacted quickly, drawing the shadows into itself and hurling forwards.

Light and dark collided. Witch and creature. One and *every*one.

Puddlebrain kept the image of her fallen friend at the forefront of her mind. She kept her hands clasped, imagining it was her hand holding his. She clung on to the hope that he was trapped and not dead. And she used that hope as a beacon.

She spoke the word again. Louder this time. With heart and meaning and rage.

"*Billy!*"

The vortex around her flared even more brightly. It became hot, the light taking on a burning intensity as it spun. It was the Multitude's turn to scream. Whether in anger or pain, Puddlebrain didn't know and couldn't care. She could feel it slipping through the barriers she was conjuring. It slid tendrils into the minutest of cracks in her defences, tendrils that seemed to lick her skin in taunting hatred. She recoiled, wavering slightly but, when she felt the Multitude attempt to grip her harder, she fought back.

"BILLY!"

There was a blast of searing heat and Puddlebrain felt as if something had reached inside her and ripped her guts out through her throat. She gagged, but held her resolve. She squeezed her hands tighter, ducked her head and clenched her teeth.

The Multitude quivered violently, its vibrations shaking the witch's jaw. There was an abrupt lull, a pause in the chaos, and the churning darkness was ripped from Puddlebrain's maelstrom. She released her hands and the whirling spread, a tsunami of radiance washing over everything. The girl fell to the floor, her arm raised over her head in defence.

"Don't hurt m…"

Her voice was, once more, that of a young girl. Innocent. Plaintive. Terrified.

She didn't finish her sentence. The tidal wave hit her and took her body with it, the girl shattering into innumerable tiny pieces and being washed away.

Puddlebrain collapsed on her knees. Her face was buried in her hands as she sobbed.

"Billy…"

"What?"

Chapter Forty One

She looked up, straight into the amused eyes of the gnome.

"You're alive?"

"I am, though I'll never dance the tango again."

"Could you tango before?"

"I've never tried."

Puddlebrain swept up her friend in her arms and pulled him in tightly. Her tears flowed freely, relief releasing them.

"Careful!" berated Billy. "I break, you know!"

"Sorry," she stammered. "Your ankle. I'm sorry."

"I've got another one. I'll be fine. Just help us out of here."

"Us?" Puddlebrain asked, frowning.

"You, me and that lot. I suppose we'd best get 'em out of this hole."

She looked past him. The cave was filled with figures but these were not shadowy ghosts of the Multitude – these were people! The villagers surrounded her, smiling but with confused expressions. She saw Brenda and Mrs. Mead and Quentin Bopsidy. At the front of the throng was her sisters. Edna stepped forward.

"Thank you," she said.

Gemini moved to stand next to the eldest witch.

"I'm hungry," she said.

Chapter Forty Two

When the world turns upside down, it has a habit of righting itself rather quickly. Quentin Bopsidy was back headmastering at the school the very next morning. Gemini's appetite hadn't abated and her toe nails were as rancid as ever.

Edna, however, had a newfound respect for her youngest sister. She started to ask Puddlebrain's advice when mixing her potions. She bit her tongue, sometimes literally, when a conversation threatened to take a turn along the sarcasm side-street. Habits were difficult to break, but she tried.

Brimley kept his magic purse a secret, but freely gave money away if he felt someone might need it. The school gained a library. Windermere, the old man who lived at the end of Shadowmoss Lane, was given a new house. It was nothing grand (Brimley was finding generosity a difficult playmate and they would often fall out), and Windermere complained it was too small to walk about on his crutches, even though it was much bigger than his rundown old shack.

Henry Pesterdear visited Gemini every other afternoon at precisely thirteen o'clock, fully laden with treats.

Billy's leg did heal, though he was correct in that he never did dance the tango. He didn't know how and never had danced at all before, so it wasn't important.

And Puddlebrain was noticed. Villagers smiled at her. Hugged her, in fact. They crossed the street to say hello rather than to avoid her.

The family of green silverfish that lived in the witches' garden continued with their own lives, oblivious to the near catastrophic events that had occurred around them.

The Grimace was not ventured in to again. Puddlebrain, for a long time, would visit its edge daily but the branches were never opened to invite her in. Thistle never greeted her. The forest remained as it had always been.

Forbidden.

Epilogue

Windermere settled into his sofa and rested his crutches against the arm. He was tired. He loved his new home, though he refused to admit as much, but it had been designed for someone much younger and so much more agile than he was.

He looked out of his window at the witches' house. He smiled. In the corners of his room, the shadows swirled. In the corners of his eyes, the shadows thickened.

Under the bed in the room directly above his lounge, a dark spot was spreading across the floor.

The End

About the Author

Shaun Allan is a bestselling, award winning author who writes multiple genres, including psychological horror, introspective and emotive poetry, young adult and children's. He has appeared on Sky TV to debate publishing, is a Wattpad Creator and Adim Founding Creator, and been commissioned to write companion stories for such movies as The Purge: Anarchy, Sinister II, The Boy, A Quiet Place, IT and Amazon Prime's Panic series. He also holds regular writing workshops at local schools. Many of his personal experiences are woven into the points of view and senses of humour of his characters, along with the places in and around his home town. His novel Sin has been adapted into a Chapters mobile game titled Straitjacket Lover. and was optioned for television.

Shaun lives with his manic dog, Ripley (believe it or not). He works full time and, though his life feels as hyper as his dog, it probably isn't.

You can read more from Shaun at:

www.shaunallan.co.uk

Facebook/Instagram/Threads/TikTok: @singularityspoint

X: @singularityspnt

MORE BOOKS BY THE AUTHOR

Sin

MirrorMirror

Cell

Pieces of Me

A Child Called Wendy

And the Meek Shall Walk

Dorthy

Dark Places

Darker Places

Printed in Great Britain
by Amazon

47641239R00118